Eva G Bjertnes was born in Bergen, Norway and has spent the last thirty years living in London. She has been an international model, a police woman, a TV presenter and now works in retail.

Opposites is Eva's very first novel and is an unconventional love story which she finished while being furloughed during lockdown.

Eva G Bjertnes

OPPOSITES

AUSTIN MACAULEY PUBLISHERS™

LONDON ∗ CAMBRIDGE ∗ NEW YORK ∗ SHARJAH

A CIP catalogue record for this title is available from the British Library.

ISBN 9781398431669 (Paperback)
ISBN 9781398431676 (ePub e-book)

www.austinmacauley.com

First Published 2022
Austin Macauley Publishers Ltd®
1 Canada Square
Canary Wharf
London
E14 5AA

I would like to thank my sister Lilian for faithfully reading chapter by chapter as I was writing the final draft and gave me a valuable feedback and who always supports me in everything I do. My friend Claire for being my weekly support buddy and still is, and my friend Malgosia who encouraged me to put a deadline on finishing the book and constantly encouraged me to find a publisher.

Chapter One

It was New York City in the middle of May 1932, and Sarah had been living in the same neighbourhood all her life, and she didn't know why she had never seen him before? Mind you, today she actually was about a twenty-five-minute walk away from her house. He, the man in question, was one of the top mob leaders, but that was not what she saw.

It was strange, because she didn't normally leave the house at that time of the evening. But on this particular day, her client had insisted on taking her out for a very special meal, and the client Margaret Wilson had not taken no for an answer. And interestingly, on that evening, she had not received any bookings! None at all!

The spirits had wanted her to go out that evening, she realised much later on. Her client, Margaret Wilson, and Sarah ate at the Italian restaurant, Romanos, in the neighbourhood which was home to most of the mob. Why Margaret had chosen that particular restaurant, Sarah didn't know.

They had a pleasant meal and didn't speak about anything of any significance, and Sarah was none the wiser why Margaret had invited her out in the first place. After the meal, they said their goodbyes outside the restaurant, and Margaret started walking in the opposite direction to Sarah.

As Sarah started to walk in the direction of her house, a car slowed down next to her, and she heard a voice saying, "This is no place for a dame like you on her own, this time of night." Sarah turned and looked as the car stopped and she could see his face in the backseat, she couldn't make out the face of his driver.

She recognised him as one of the men who had dined at the restaurant, she knew he was one of the leaders from the way the others had treated him. What she couldn't work out was his looks. He was very good-looking, tall, blonde, blue-eyed, probably Irish, so how had he gotten in with the mob? The rest of them were short, dark-haired, brown-eyed Italians.

He had a cheeky grin on his face as he was taking her in. Sarah was not afraid of him, the night or the neighbourhood. She knew she was safe anywhere, and if she should ever be in danger, the spirits would let her know. So she simply asked, "Says who?"

"I do," he said.

"And who are you, may I ask?" Sarah asked.

"John O'Connor," he replied, still with a cocky attitude. "I haven't seen you around here before, may I have your name?" he asked not taking his eyes off her.

"My name is Sarah Steel, and no, I don't tend to hang around this part of the neighbourhood, that's probably why you haven't seen me before," Sarah replied.

"Well, I am very sorry to hear that you don't come this way very often, but that is something I would like to rectify. And let me start by taking you home."

"Well, if it makes you feel better by doing that, who am I to argue," Sarah said. John's driver opened the door for her and she got in the car next to John O'Connor in the back seat. He didn't scare or intimidate her, which amused John.

"A woman with balls," he thought, "I like that."

All Sarah saw was a young boy in a man's body, enjoying the power and attention he got, while playing a very dangerous game in the world. They sat in silence, Sarah looking out the window, quite relaxed and in her own thoughts. She still couldn't work out why Margaret had taken her out for dinner that evening, as nothing specific had been said about anything.

John, on the other hand, was looking at her in amusement, with a big smile on his face. John knew that Sarah, in that moment, was totally unaware of him, and he was amazed. No one was ever unaware of his presence, or so he thought until now.

How could she not be afraid of him; how could she not be aware of his presence? For the first time in his adult life, he found himself speechless!

And what was it about her that had him feel unnerved? He had to find out! Sarah broke the silence.

"Do you know where I live? Or do you need directions?" Sarah directed the question at the driver. John felt as if all his power had been taken away.

"How dare she address Oscar and not me, this is my car and I am in charge!"

Oscar replied to Sarah, "No, I am afraid I don't know where we are going, Ma'am, so I would appreciate an address or directions please."

John was stunned, now Oscar had made him look a complete fool, as he had failed to obtain from Sarah where they were going. For a moment, he felt invisible, not a great feeling, he was furious. Sarah told Oscar where to go and slipped back into her own thoughts.

John composed himself and said, "I apologise, I should have made sure I knew where we were going when you got in the car. I was just so blinded by your beauty, I stopped thinking for a moment," John smiled his best smile, trying a charm offence.

"That's okay, Mr O'Connor, it was my mistake, as I should have said when I got in the car. How could you possibly know where I live?" What amazed him the most about her speaking was that there was no sarcasm or attitude, just a plain statement. And it was completely neutral, if there was such a thing.

Before he could think of anything else to say, they had arrived outside Sarah's house. It was very light and lovely looking, "just like her," he thought. She was a very striking looking woman, tall, blonde with the greenest eyes he had ever seen. Her hair was shoulder length, soft and wavy, and she was slim with curves in all the right places.

"Oh," Sarah suddenly realised they were outside her house. "Thank you for the lift, it was very kind of you," she said as she jumped out of the car, not waiting for Oscar or John to open the door for her. She had an energetic lightweight manner in which she moved, which made John smile. She was like a breath of fresh air compared to most of the women he knew.

She was out of the car and on the sidewalk before John had a chance to do or say anything. At that point, he was trying to compose himself again and act cool and said, "Anytime, Lady," but his voice almost cracked and he felt about thirteen years old.

"Get home safely now," Sarah said and waved. Like he needed protection!

Who the hell did she think she was! He felt angry and humiliated at the same time, and Oscar, his driver, was looking very amused. He had never, in all the years he had known his boss since he had become an adult, seen him lose his cool or confidence with anyone ever. But he had to admit, that dame was something else. She was not scared of nothing.

She would have walked home alone, and he was certain nothing would have happened to her. She just had that way about her.

Then John noticed his grin and screamed, "What the hell are you looking at? Move the fucking car!"

Wow, the big boss had gone totally wobbly over a dame. He'd better keep it to himself, any sign of weakness could be dangerous at this moment in time, at any time really. So, Oscar put on his professional face again, and pretended that had not seen anything.

He had known John since he was a boy and would protect him at all cost. Then, something occurred to him, the woman that Sarah Steel had been dining with this evening, Margaret Wilson, had been an informant for them for quite some time. And recently, they had found out that she had been "friendly" with the police too.

And she had got very cocky in the last few months, acting like she was invincible. And tonight was the night when the boss had "arranged" for Margaret Wilson, to be taken care of. So, John must have wanted to get Sarah home safely, and at the same time, check her out to see if she knew anything or was involved in anything.

Oscar had seen a lot of dodgy people over the years from all walks of life, and he was a pretty good judge of character, and he was prepared to bet his life on, that Sarah Steel had never been involved in anything dodgy in her entire life. Why? Because she didn't pretend in anything she did, she was straight as an arrow.

Oscar was ripped away from his thoughts when he heard John his boss calling out, "Are you deaf? I have been asking you the same question three times. What time is it, and do I have anything else on the schedule for tonight?"

"11.30pm boss, and no, nothing else on the schedule for tonight."

"Good, take me home, I am going to have an early night for a change." Oscar was completely gob-smacked, his boss would normally hit at least two bars a night before he turned in at 2 or 3 am. For once, John was on his own, which was very rare. And he just couldn't get Sarah out of his head.

He had noticed her the minute she had walked into the restaurant, for the exact opposite reason why you would normally notice someone. She did not draw any attention to herself, and she had this quiet grace about her, which was the exact thing that had him sit up and take notice.

Most of the women in his circles were loud and vulgar and tried to get as much attention as possible, which he had always found unattractive. It was also the fact that she seemed so comfortable in her own skin, and that she didn't "need" the attention or want it at all.

During the meal, she had not been looking around the room to see if anyone was paying her any attention, she had studied the menu, chatted with her friend, ordered her meal and been very friendly and polite to the waiters. In that particular restaurant, most of the women who came in were either mistresses of the men who frequented the place, occasionally the wives, or women looking for a man with money in his pocket.

He realised that he had not been able to take his eyes off her the entire time she was there, and had made sure Oscar had got the car ready before she left, so that he could catch her as she left. He was also intrigued by the "friendship" between Margaret Wilson and Sarah Steel, such an unlikely combination.

He thought he knew everyone that Margaret would spend time with in his neighbourhood, had he gotten sloppy? Then again, Sarah lived outside of his "territory" where Margaret wouldn't usually be watched.

"So what was Sarah doing with Margaret this evening, and how would she feel when Margaret disappeared. And would she connect him with the disappearance?"

He was getting really pissed off with himself, "Why the hell should he care about what Sarah thought about anything?" He slumped down in his favourite armchair and sighed.

"What the hell is wrong with me? I haven't felt like this since I was about thirteen and had a crush on Wendy Wheeler, who didn't even know I existed. He had to pull himself together, it would be dangerous to get involved. And he didn't know how involved Sarah was in Margaret's affairs, he just couldn't work out the connection.

While he was sitting there, he worked out a plan of action. The next day when it became known that Margaret had disappeared, he would go over to Sarah's house and offer his sympathy and explain that he had known Margaret for years, and that it was terrible that she had disappeared. He was happy with his plan and went to bed, looking forward to seeing Sarah again the following day.

At 7 am, Oscar was banging on his bedroom door. John was furious, he had been in the middle of the best sleep he had had in years, and his dream had involved a certain lady.

"It better be important," he thought, and was shocked when Oscar told him what had happened. Margaret had been involved in a hit and run accident, and had then managed to drag herself to Sarah's house. Sarah had called an ambulance and Margaret had been taken to the hospital, and Sarah had gone with her.

John was totally shocked and confused. This was not how last night's events were meant to go. Also wondering how much Sarah knew, and if Margaret had recognised the car or the driver? For once in his adult life, he wasn't sure what to do. He couldn't go over to Sarah's house that early in the morning and he couldn't call the hospital or the police without looking suspicious.

He would have to wait until later that morning or early afternoon to do anything, and it would be common knowledge about what had happened to Margaret. He went back to bed, floating in and out of consciousness, having images of Sarah hovering above him in a white gown, telling him that everything was going to be alright.

He regained consciousness around 9.30 am, feeling exhausted and powerless.

"This was not how last night was meant to go. He had to pull himself together, and he asked himself, What would the "Old" John O'Connor's have done in this situation?" At 10 am, Oscar informed John that Margaret had passed away soon after arriving at the hospital, from extensive injuries including internal bleeding. And no one knew exactly what had happened as Margaret had been so badly injured she had been unable to communicate anything.

God only knew how she had managed to get herself to Sarah's house in her state, but at least now, he knew what to do, back to plan A. He would go to Sarah's house and offer his condolences, for the loss of her friend. At noon, Oscar drove John to Sarah's house. They stopped at a flower stall on the way, and got her a beautiful bouquet of flowers. And they arrived at Sarah's house soon after 12.30 pm.

There were no signs of life and the curtains were drawn. He hesitated, which wasn't normally his style. But then he thought, "I'm here now, and I want to check how she is," and with that thought, he walked up the steps to Sarah's front door and knocked gently. There was no answer.

He hesitated and knocked again, again no answer. Standing there, waiting and hoping she would open the door, he suddenly had this feeling he was being watched. He turned around and saw Sarah standing at the bottom of her stairs, looking at him with a surprised look on her face.

"What are you doing here?" she asked looking tired and drawn. To his surprise, he felt this overwhelming sense of love and compassion, and all he wanted to do was take her in his arms and look after her.

"News travels fast in this neighbourhood," he heard himself saying, "And I wanted to come and offer my condolences, for the loss of your friend."

He was surprised how quickly he had slipped back into being the John O'Connor he knew himself to be, confident and relaxed in any situation, based on years of training in the mob. Or maybe it was because she seemed so tired and vulnerable, he felt more in control of the situation again.

The next thing Sarah said, clarified things a little bit for John, "Margaret wasn't a friend; she was one of my clients."

He tried to hide his relief and then couldn't help but ask, "Do you normally go out to dinner with your clients?"

"No," Sarah said as she unlocked the front door, and added, "Last night was a one off, I have never been out with a client before, ever. But Margaret had really insisted on taking me out, and wouldn't take no for an answer."

"Oh," he said, "That is very intriguing." Sarah turned and looked at him, with a very intense look in her eyes. And he regretted the choice of his last few words. It felt like she could see right through him, and that she knew everything about him.

"You better come in," she said and let him in through the front door. She took him straight into her parlour. Her house was very beautiful, yet very simple. It was neat and tidy with very light coloured furniture and décor, and she obviously loved lace because there was a fair amount of it around her parlour. The net curtains and all the table cloths were all lace.

The more he looked around the room, the more he saw Sarah in every piece of furniture, fittings and ornaments. And there was a huge picture of an angel on the wall, with a beautiful angelic face, and a plain white robe and huge wings.

Golden curly hair, floating in the air, with blue sky and surrounded by soft cotton balls of clouds. A picture of perfect divine bliss, and he also noticed how comfortable and peaceful he felt in her parlour.

"Please take a seat," Sarah said, breaking through the silence. John looked around wondering where to sit. She had a large sofa by her dining table and two very comfortable looking arm chairs by the window, facing the street with a small table in between. John decided to sit in one of the arm chairs.

"Let me get us a drink," Sarah said.

"It's a bit early for liquor, isn't it," John said.

"I meant a tea or a coffee," Sarah replied, slightly impatient.

"Oh," John said going bright red. Jesus Christ, he had completely lost his cool again. And he felt like a price idiot. Why was it that he couldn't keep his cool for more than a couple of minutes at the time, with this woman? Sarah was standing in the middle of the floor of her parlour, looking at him with a question mark on her face.

"Tea or coffee," she asked him again.

He went bright red again, cleared his throat and said, "Coffee please, black, thank you," and he looked down like an embarrassed child. I have to pull myself together; I can't carry on like this. I will lose all my street cred and put myself and her in danger, acting like a lovesick fool! Then something strange happened to him, he felt this enormous urge to just be himself, no façade, no Mr Tough guy, just him plain and simple. But he knew that with his line of work, that was almost impossible, unless he had a death wish.

In spite of his very last thoughts, by the time Sarah came back into the parlour, he was completely relaxed. And he felt so incredibly comfortable in her house. He knew this could be dangerous for Sarah, but in this moment, he didn't want to think about that.

As Sarah walked back into the parlour he thought to himself, "She really is the most beautiful woman!" It wasn't just her physical appearance that made her beautiful, she also had an aura around her that made her shine and it was absolutely mesmerising.

She was like an angel or a new born baby that has this pure innocent energy that everyone is attracted to. That was it! She was divine! And for a moment, he felt like a small child that just wanted to be held by this beautiful woman.

John O'Connor's had a soft spot, and her name was Sarah Steel. Sarah put the tray down on the dining table and came and stood directly in front of him.

"Are they for me?" she asked pointing at the flowers. He felt this warm smile come over him, as he handed her the flowers.

"Thank you," she said, "They are beautiful."

"That's my pleasure," John replied.

And for the first time in a long time, he actually meant it. He would pay a lot more than the price of a bouquet of flowers, to see that smile on her face again. Suddenly he was not worried about anything, he was just enjoying being with her, in her surroundings.

Sarah took the flowers and disappeared into what he assumed was the kitchen, while he was imagining what it would be like to live there with her.

Normally, that kind of thought would have shocked him, but today it felt like a really nice day dream.

Sarah came back, put the flowers on the dining table in a very pretty vase, which was in the same style as the rest of the room. Sarah then poured him a coffee in a pretty china cup, and walked over, and gave it to him. She then poured herself a cup of herbal tea and came and sat down in the other arm chair.

"So, what is it that I can do for you Mr O'Connor?" she asked. The words took him by surprise, it also burst the bubble of day dreaming he had been sitting in. And this awkward lack of confidence came over him again. He had let his guard down for a moment and he was not prepared for her question. So he allowed himself some time to think before he answered her question.

"It's not what you can do for me Miss Steel, but what I can possibly do for you. I was concerned for you when I heard about your friend's, eh, client's death and wanted to offer my support," John said in reply to her question.

"Oh, but there is no need, like I said, Margaret was a client, not a close friend and I'm sure her family will take care of everything."

"Family," he thought. He never knew that Margaret had any family!

Sarah had seen the surprise on his face and said, "I thought you knew her better than me?"

"What gave you that impression?" John replied trying to sound as casual as possible.

"Oh, a woman's intuition," she replied.

"Yes of course," John said. "If you don't mind me asking, what exactly is it that you do Miss Steel? In what way was Margaret a client of yours?" John asked as innocently as he could.

"Oh sorry, of course you don't know what I do. I am a psychic medium, and I do readings for people," Sarah replied in a very matter of fact way, as though that was the most natural thing in the world to do. And secretly, he was thinking, this woman can see people's futures, their pasts and that is more than just a woman's intuition. How much did she know?

Never mind, she had let him into her house and she didn't seem to have any issues with him. So he was just going to enjoy her company and her space for now. They sat in silence for a while and it was really comfortable. For him any way, he couldn't really speak for Sarah. He had not experienced anything like this for a very, very long time. Not since he was a young boy and his mother and him would sit and read together in their parlour.

Sarah seemed lost in her own thoughts and John was glancing over at her as much as he could, without being too obvious.

"God, she is breath-taking. Was he, John, in with a chance?" he had never thought that he would get to a point where he was actually questioning whether a woman would want him or not. He had never been short of women. As a matter of fact, women had always been throwing themselves at him. And he had used them and "abused" them like a disposable commodity. He could never do that to Sarah. Never!

For the first time in his adult life he was unsure about everything in his life. His past, his present and his future, he who had been so clear about it all ever since his parents died.

"It's not easy when life throws you a wildcard, is it?" Sarah broke the silence. He jumped at her words.

"Was Sarah talking about herself of him? Could she actually read his mind?" "He had never felt so naked in his whole life! Are you talking about Margaret?" he managed to say.

"Yes of course, what did you think I was talking about?" Sarah asked.

"I just wasn't sure," John replied feeling extremely calm as he said it, which was a great relief for him.

"I really am quite tired, I had a very long night, and would like to try and get some sleep, if you don't mind." Sarah said in a very plain and gentle manner.

"Yes of course!" John was on his feet in a flash and apologised for being so insensitive. He could not believe the stuff that was coming out of his mouth. He had not apologised to anyone since his mother was alive. But everything was different with Sarah, and as he left her house he was chuckling to himself.

"Well, well, well John, you have fallen for her and that is just the way it is." And he was actually beginning to enjoy the feeling.

"Now there was a man who had chosen a path for himself that had never been right for him," Sarah thought as she closed the door behind him.

Chapter Two

Three days had passed and he had not been able to come up with an excuse to go and see Sarah again.

"But when you least expect it, something happens that you had not foreseen," he thought to himself. Sarah turned up at his house unannounced on the fourth day, while John was having a meeting with his guys. Oscar had let her in and taken her into John's study, and asked her if she would like anything to drink, which she declined. Then Oscar informed John that he had a visitor.

John's jaw dropped in surprise, but he pulled himself together quickly so his guys wouldn't notice. Then he told Oscar not to let her leave until he had a chance to see her. From the moment he knew that Sarah was in his house, he could not concentrate on anything else.

So he wrapped up the meeting with his guys as fast as he could, leaving them pretty unsure about what their instructions were. But they knew not to argue with him. And before he went to see her, he gave Oscar clear instructions that none of the guys were to know anything about Sarah's identity.

"Yes boss that goes without saying," Oscar replied to his instructions. John got up as soon as his guys were out the door, checked himself in the mirror and "put" on his professional 'I am in charge' look, walked down the hall, and opened the door to his study feeling confident and strong. But as soon as he saw her it hit him right in the gut and he felt an urge to go to the toilet.

Sarah got up as soon as he walked through the door, and he immediately gestured for her to sit down again with a polite "please" and an arm movement. He didn't know whether to remain standing or sit down. He wanted to stand to try and keep some of his authority, but at the same time he felt a bit wobbly. So, in the end, he decided to sit down, also partly because he felt it would be a bit rude to hover over her.

"Miss Steel, how nice to see you again, to what do I owe this pleasure?" He said.

"Forgive me in advance if what I am about to ask you is inappropriate," Sarah began looking slightly uncomfortable, which was very unlike her.

"Miss Steel, I cannot imagine that you would ever ask anyone anything inappropriate," he replied with a gentle smile trying to put her at ease.

"You haven't heard what I am about to ask you yet," Sarah quickly jumped in to say, looking a little more confident. He was glad he had made her feel a bit more at ease.

"I don't know if you were aware that Margaret Wilson had a family?" she asked him.

"Family?" He said pretty shocked and before he could stop himself he added, "She kept that very quiet!"

"Yes it would seem so," Sarah said with a sigh and carried on. "Margaret was a single mother of two lovely boys aged seven and ten, and I have just found out that there is no money to pay for the funeral. And that is why, I am here to ask if you would be willing to pay for some of the funeral expenses?"

He had to hand it to her; this woman really did have balls. She had not hesitated to come to one of the biggest mob bosses in the area asking for money for a woman who had been a double agent, so to speak, and had worked against him on many an occasion as far as he knew. But then again, he didn't know how much Sarah knew about Margaret's life at all.

"Don't worry," he said, "I will pay for everything."

"No, that is not necessary, I have a little bit of money put away and…" John put his hand up and stopped her mid-sentence.

"Miss Steel, I would not dream of you paying for any of it. For a person who was just a client of yours," he said.

"Thank you Mr O'Connor, that is very generous of you," Sarah replied. The way she said his name even though she was using his second name, sent shivers through his whole body and he really had a problem keeping up his authoritative stature. They fell silent, but he could tell there was more. That Sarah wasn't done yet.

"What else can I do for you, Miss Steel?" He said wanting to make it easier for her.

"It is Mrs Steel, actually," Sarah said plainly.

"You are married?" John said finding it hard not to show his feelings of shock and pain in his gut and heart.

"I was," Sarah said, "I am a widow now."

"You are far too young to be a widow," he said without thinking.

"Yes," she said, "but sometimes, life gives you situations that you just did not expect."

"I am so sorry," John said and really, really meant it.

"Thank you," Sarah replied. He had never known such a genuine straight forward person before, who had obviously been through a lot and did not have a hint of self-pity. She had simply stated a fact.

"Regarding Margaret's two boys," she said, "I shipped them off the morning Margaret passed away to my sister and her husband in the country temporarily. They have a farm and are fairly comfortable, but any help would be greatly appreciated." He would have given her the whole world if she had asked for it, regardless of who it was for.

"I will set up a trust fund for both of them and a monthly allowance," he said.

"Thank you so much, you have no idea what this entire thing means to me," Sarah said.

"Anytime, I mean it. If you ever need anything, you come to me!" John said in a very firm voice.

"You are a very kind man, John O'Connor," Sarah replied looking relieved. The way she said his name had him completely melt inside. And at the same time he was thinking, "kind?" no one else in the whole world thought of him as kind as far as he knew.

"I think you must be mistaking me for someone else, Mrs Steel," he said and smiled.

"Please, call me Sarah," she said.

"Okay Sarah, would you like me to take care of the funeral arrangements or would you like to do it?" John asked.

"Oh, I couldn't possibly ask you to do that after you have already been so generous and kind," Sarah replied.

"I tell you what, why don't we do it together, Sarah?" John said.

"Okay," she replied and smiled. And he could again see the relief on her face. This poor beautiful woman had been dragged into a situation that had really been none of her business, and she had taken it on with such grace.

"Good, now that that has been agreed, I am going to buy you lunch," John declared.

"Thank you that would be very nice," Sarah responded. He had already ordered from Romanos.

"We will eat in the dining room," John said as he got up and opened the door and gesturing for Sarah to go through first. Sarah got up quietly and gracefully and walked past him through the door.

"Down the hall, second on your right," John explained. He watched her walking in front of him and he had to control himself, because he felt very strong urges that he had not felt in years, desires mixed with real emotions.

As they approached the dining room door he slipped past her and opened the door for her. His housekeeper Rose, Oscar's wife had set a beautiful table with his best china and silver ware. Good old Rose, he could always rely on her to do a great job. Oscar was his driver and right hand man and he lived with Rose in the top floor apartment of John's house.

Oscar and Rose had worked for John for a very long time and they were almost like parents to him, although he would never admit to that. And they both secretly treated him like a son who had got a bit lost. And Oscar had told Rose that this "new" woman was very different from all of John's other women in the past, and that John had literally lost the plot over her.

"She must be something very special then, Rose had thought, and I will treat her accordingly." It still very much amused Oscar that John O'Connor, the big boss himself, had fallen head over heels for a dame. But this time Oscar very much approved of the dame. He was more concerned that John would get Sarah into trouble than the other way around.

John walked over to the table and pulled out a chair for Sarah, and enjoyed watching her making her way towards him.

"My god, where has this woman been all of my life?" he asked himself. He then went and sat opposite her, and he felt her eyes on him as he walked around the table. He gave her a smile as he sat down, finally feeling back in control of himself.

"I don't know what you like so I ordered a few things from the menu, but if I had known you were coming, I would have got Rose, my housekeeper, to cook for us, she is an amazing cook," John said.

"It looks lovely," Sarah said, "I think I would like to try the meatballs."

"Very well, meatballs it is," John said grabbed the bowl with the meatballs and went over to serve her. There were a lot of firsts, going on for John. One of them was, he had never served anyone at his dining table before. They either helped themselves or Rose did it. But he had made it clear that he wanted to dine with Sarah alone.

Rose was silently overjoyed that John had finally fallen in love with someone that could possibly be very good for him. Rose looked upon John as a son and worried about him constantly, and this was the first time she felt that something good was happening to him. So she was very happy to leave the two of them alone.

John was constantly surprising himself. What a softie he had become in Sarah's presence. A smile on her face or a look of appreciation completely melted his heart, and there was nothing he could do about it. Sarah always enjoyed her food and it gave John great pleasure watching her tucking in.

They ate in silence and it felt natural and comfortable for both of them. "How was he going to win this woman over?" his mind was wondering while they ate. Things that would normally impress other women seemed to have no effect on Sarah at all. But he had noticed that generosity and kindness went a long way. And as he thought about that, he realised it wasn't hard to be like that when she was around.

On the other hand, he was concerned with the fact that she didn't approve of what he did for a "living," as far as she approved or disapproved of anyone. He got the impression that she didn't really judge anyone, but that didn't mean she would be willing to be "involved" with him. "Oh man, I just can't think of anything but her. What she might think, what she might like and what she might not like."

It was completely unknown territory for him, and there was a huge part of him that didn't like this new way of feeling and thinking at all!

"Thank you so much, that was just what I needed, a good wholesome meal," Sarah said looking more relaxed.

"I'm glad you enjoyed it, and I am happy to repeat this anytime you are hungry and don't feel like cooking," John said with a huge grin on his face.

Sarah smiled too, and said, "That is a very generous offer John." And there it was again, that sting in his heart when she said his name.

"I don't know yet when the police are going to release Margaret's body, because they are still investigating the accident. But as soon as I know, I will let you know," she said. John didn't quite know how to respond to her statement. He thought about what should have happened that night, but then again Sarah wouldn't have known that, or would she?

So he said, "The whole thing is very sad and yes as soon as you know, please inform me and we can give her a decent send-off." He wanted to say, "But I hope

I will see you before then." But it didn't seem appropriate given what they were talking about.

"I have taken a lot of your time, so I shall leave you in peace," Sarah said and stood up.

"It has been an absolute pleasure seeing you again Sarah, I just wish it could have been under better circumstances. And as I have said before, anything you need, anything at all, I'm your man," he said feeling on a real high after spending time with her.

Sarah looked a little bit uncomfortable after his "speech," and he wished he had toned it down a bit. Well, it was too late to take it back but he added, "I am sorry if I made you feel uncomfortable, that was not my intention."

Sarah blushed slightly and said, "Don't worry, you have been very kind, and I'm not quite myself today. I am feeling a little tired still after the other night."

"Yes of course. Let me get Oscar to take you home in the car," John replied.

"No, no, the walk will do me good" Sarah insisted.

With lifted eyebrows John said, "That is a very long walk, are you sure?" Suddenly a shadow came over her face and he could see how tired she was.

Sarah changed her mind and said, "Actually, I will take you up on your offer, I don't think I have the energy to walk all the way back as well."

"You walked here?" he asked.

"Yes I did," she replied.

"Right I will fetch Oscar straight away," he said and disappeared out of the room. While John was gone, Sarah glanced around the room. She hadn't really noticed it earlier; her eyes had been focused on the beautiful laid out table and the lovely food. The room was big as she would probably have expected it to be, considering his "position". But it was much simpler than she had imagined.

Everything was elegant and understated and very much reflected the "real" him, she thought. She had already on their first meeting realised that underneath the tough guy, I'm in charge, façade, there was a lovely little lost boy who would not harm a fly.

She wondered what had happened to him that had made him choose the path he had chosen. There was always a reason she thought, always. She did also suspect that he was behind Margaret's "accident" and that he now felt really bad about it and wanted to make amends. And she knew that at some point, she would know the whole truth, but for the moment, she wasn't going to judge anyone.

"Always find out the facts before you judge anyone Sarah," her father had taught her. And whatever John had done, was between him and his maker, it was the same for everyone, although society didn't always see it that way. Underneath it all, John was such a kind and generous man, and at the moment he was working so hard to put everything right by giving her the help she needed.

She could have gone elsewhere and asked for help, she knew a lot of wealthy people, but she had chosen him because she knew she could trust him. And because she felt it would do him a lot of good, giving Margaret a proper send off. She had been so deep in thought that she didn't hear John come back into the room. She did have a habit of doing that; disappear into her own world and the rest of the world disappearing around her.

"Right, Oscar is ready whenever you are," John said. Sarah looked up.

"Thank you, I am ready." John escorted her to the anonymous car at the back of the house where there was a secret court yard, which led to an alley way that was not "connected" to his house, which he used when he didn't want anyone to see someone leaving his house. He hoped no one had seen her arrive earlier for her own safety.

Anyone associated with him, that the opposition might think was of value to him, they could try to harm to get to him. No one knew how close he was to Oscar and Rose, so as far as everybody was concerned they were just staff and of no importance to him beyond that.

He made sure Sarah got safely inside the car and said, "I am sorry I won't be able to escort you back, but you are in safe hands with Oscar. And I took the liberty of packing some of the food that was left over for you. It's right here on the seat, and will save you from having to cook for yourself tonight. In the parcel, you will find my number, so call as soon as you have any news." And with that, he shut closed the car door and waved her off. And he felt that sharp pain in his heart again, seeing her leave.

He had chosen not to go with her, when Oscar took her home, as he knew it would have been incredibly difficult for him to keep calm and collected in the back seat next to her. And he wasn't ready to be vulnerable or rejected or both, just yet.

He had almost convinced himself that Sarah would never be interested in a man like him, not because of who he was but because of what he did. Actually, to her, that probably was one and the same thing. His doing would for her overshadow his being. This was completely new territory for him and he felt completely out of his dept.

"What did she think of him?" He had no idea. She was the kind of person who would treat everyone the same, so it was impossible to know what she thought of anyone in particular.

Oscar was dying to ask Mrs Steel a million questions, especially what she thought about his boss, but was wise enough to stay silent. He had never seen John like this before with a woman, and he did not want to ruin any development if he could help it. This woman Sarah Steel, he did not want to scare away.

When they arrived outside Sarah's house, he quickly got out of the car, opened the door for her and grabbed the food parcel and carried it to her front door.

"Have a nice evening ma'am," he said and wanted to add, "any time you need a lift anywhere, I'm your man, I will make sure of it," but he didn't.

In some ways, he was as smitten as John was, he thought and chuckled to himself.

"Better not tell Rose that," he thought and chuckled again.

"Well, at least this woman puts a smile on people's faces," he thought as he got back in the car.

"Thank you very much, you are so sweet," Sarah said.

Oscar smiled and said, "Any time." He knew that when a woman said you were sweet, they liked you or what you were doing or offering, and this was one lady he wanted to keep sweet. Oscar and Rose had been looking out for John since he was sixteen and his parents had disappeared.

No one knew what had happened to them, although he sometimes had the distinct impression that John did, but John never spoke about it. Until that day when John's parents had disappeared, John had been a sweet young man, polite and shy, never getting into any trouble. But overnight, he had changed completely.

He stayed out all night; he started drinking and often returned home with a black eye or worse. But he must have soon learned to fight, because it didn't take long before he returned home without a bloody face, only blood on his knuckles and hands. So he was obviously starting to give the punches rather than receiving them.

The house John was living in had belonged to his parents, and his father had been a very successful business man. And that was why John O'Connor's house

24

was situated away from the rest of the mob. And he was also very well spoken even for an Irish man, which had always surprised his opponents.

Why John had chosen the path he had, Oscar didn't know or wasn't sure of although he had his suspicions. What he had heard was the rumours that the mob wanted security money from John's father and his father had refused point blank time and time again, and that the mob had threatened to kill him.

Knowing too much in this town was dangerous, so Oscar always pretended to know nothing. And he was "known" for being a bit "simple". Oscar didn't mind as long as it kept him, Rose and "his boy" safe. John didn't become a raging mad gangster like many of the others in the mob.

John became ice-cold and calculated which was really scary to watch. Most people didn't argue with John, they avoided him instead. When he went ice-cold people froze, and no one could win an argument with him. But that dame, Sarah Steel, had completely melted his heart, and it was a joy to see that side of him again after all these years. But there was also a danger in it.

No one could find out about this "weakness" or both John and especially Sarah could be in danger. But Oscar knew that John knew that, as he had seen today when John made sure that Sarah left by the back entrance of the house. And he was certain that was also why John had offered Sarah lunch at the house today rather than taking her out somewhere, that and the fact that he probably wanted her all to himself.

John had even asked Rose to stay out of the way, even though she would normally have served the food and kept an eye on everything. Oscar smiled to himself; it was so nice to see John happy again he thought. And although John could be very hard to deal with sometimes, Oscar would never leave him as he had promised his parents that if anything happened to them, he and Rose would always look out for him.

Chapter Three

The next few days was rather uneventful for Sarah, it was business as usual so to speak. She had clients throughout the day and evening, and in her spare time she would read, meditate or eat her meals as normal. And she also always tried to get some fresh air everyday by taking a stroll around the nearest park.

None of her clients had mentioned Margaret, and Sarah was pleased about that. It was obvious that no one in her neighbourhood had known who Margaret was, nor what she had been up to or what had happened to her. So life was pretty normal, apart from the fact that she was waiting for the all clear from the police, that they were ready to release Margaret's body.

And from time to time, she found herself going over in her mind that evening with Margaret, and what had happened later on when Margaret had turned up at her house bloody and battered, hardly able to speak.

How Margaret had managed to get herself to Sarah's house was a mystery. It was either sheer will power or someone must have helped her. Well, it didn't matter now, she tried to kid herself, but deep down, she wondered what had really happened and who was involved. But whatever the truth was, "May Margaret's soul rest in peace," she thought.

Margaret had been a client of hers on and off for some time, she couldn't quite remember if it was two or three years or more. And they never used to talk much whenever Margaret came, Margaret had wanted a reading and that was it. But at the last few visits, Margaret had tried to be a bit friendlier and even asked Sarah some questions about her life.

Sarah preferred to stay neutral with her clients, but she was always polite and steered the conversation in a different direction. Sarah knew that Margaret had a troubled life; she had seen it again and again in her readings. And she had been very straight with her, that if she carried on doing what she was doing it would not end well.

And Margaret had said, "I know, I know but what is the solution?"

And Sarah had said, "Start a new life somewhere else, away from here." Margaret had turned up on her doorstep one day without an appointment and asked if she could come in. Sarah wasn't particularly happy about it as she really valued her alone time and her privacy.

But Margaret reassured her it would only take a minute, Sarah had let her in and taken her through to the study where she would normally sit for a reading, at the back of the house next to the kitchen. It had been her father's study and she was very comfortable in there.

Her father had been a much grounded man and Sarah needed that grounded energy to do what she did. Her father had chosen that room as his study because he liked being near his wife where he could hear her pottering around in the kitchen. It made him happy and her mother too, they had never been very far away from each other.

Once Margaret and Sarah had sat down, (Sarah had not offered Margaret anything to drink as she didn't want her to get too comfortable and stay too long), Margaret told her that she really appreciated Sarah's readings and advice and as a thank you she wanted to take Sarah out for dinner.

Sarah told her that that was not necessary, and explained to Margaret that she had already paid her for her time. But Margaret had insisted. So they had agreed a time and place, and the restaurant had been Margaret's choice. That's how Sarah had ended up at the restaurant Romanos that night when Margaret was run down and died.

Sarah was certain that it was murder, and she "knew" John O'Connor had something to do with it, even if he wasn't directly involved. The night Margaret was run down and managed to get to Sarah's place, Margaret had told Sarah a few things.

Margaret had told Sarah that she was an "informant" for the police and at the same time, she had been a pigeon for several mob bosses including John O'Connor. Basically, a double agent and she believed that neither the police nor the mob knew that she was a double agent.

This had been going well until the police department had contacted her and put pressure on her to keep them informed about certain people's movements at all times. Margaret had told Sarah that she didn't have much choice in the matter when it came to the police. The police had offered up very subtle threats, but if she cooperated, they would reward her with state allowances.

So from that point onwards, she knew she was in deep trouble. The police would keep a close eye on her, and if any of her other employers found out she was also involved with the police, she would be dead. And she knew that Sarah was the kind of person who would take care of her boys if anything was to happen to her.

She had apologised for putting all of that on Sarah, especially since they didn't really know each other that well. Margaret had also told Sarah that if she needed support, if the worst happened, that John O'Connor was the one to ask for help.

She had said that John was a very good man underneath the cold façade. That he had a big heart, which most people didn't know about. That he was always fair, but made sure that people knew there always were consequences for their actions so that they knew he wasn't to be messed with. And that most people had enormous respect for him.

Margaret had said that if John had been a cop, he would have been a straight one. Margaret had even asked Sarah if it was at all possible to "save" John from the world he was in, to do everything in her power to do so. As Margaret didn't believe that John really belonged in that world, which to Sarah, was a very strange thing to say.

Why would she want a man saved who was one of the likely suspects who had "taken care of" her "accident?" Sarah wished she had never got mixed up in this whole business, she just wanted to get back to normal, but it was too late for that.

Margaret had originally started off offering a little bit of information to mob members from time to time, of what she saw going on in their neighbourhood. Begging for a little bit of cash for her troubles, to keep herself and her boys from starving after her husband died.

She never told anyone about her boys as she wanted to keep them safe and she was able to keep them a secret because she didn't live in the neighbourhood she was "working" in. She had been perfect for the job as a "harmless" poor immigrant widow walking the streets of the neighbourhood going about her "daily business."

And as she turned out to be very good at "spying" in her harmless, innocent way, the mob started using her more and more for small things. And she earned enough to keep herself and her boys from starving and being homeless.

Chapter Four

John was restless. Ideally, he would have loved to go away to his little hideaway place up by the lakes, but he couldn't while he was waiting for Sarah to get back to him regarding the funeral arrangements. He wanted to be on hand if Sarah should need him. And the thought of being "away" from her did not feel good either.

What a mess the whole Margaret thing was, and now his complete obsession with Sarah. Half the time he felt as if he couldn't think straight. He had to pull himself together which he was telling himself a lot lately, a completely new concept for him.

He would either have to stay put and be restless or take some kind of action. And then the idea came to him. He would invite Sarah up to the lakes as an offer of getting away for a good rest for a few days, before she had to deal with the police and the release of Margaret's body.

He had to find a way to offer this that didn't seem like a sleazy invitation. And another thing he had to look out for, was that it wouldn't be in his or Sarah's interests to have the police know they were going off together for a short break.

But before he could work all that out, he had a phone call from Sarah saying that the police had been in touch and Margaret's body would not be released for at least two weeks, while they were investigating a few things. While they were on the phone, his heart was racing, but he managed to very calmly ask her if he could call on her in the next couple of days to see how she was doing.

Sarah was a little hesitant and asked him to let her know in advance if he was coming as she might be with a client. And she reassured him that she was fine, but he could hear the slightest sigh as she was speaking, indicating to him some stress or tiredness.

He told her he didn't wish to impose, but that he felt that Margaret had put an enormous responsibility on her shoulders and he just wanted to help in any way he could to ease the pressure of that for her. And he found himself genuinely meaning what he said.

Sarah thanked him kindly, but it was clear that she didn't want to talk anymore. So he came off the phone wishing her a pleasant day. And again, he found himself wondering what his next move was going to be. He didn't want to add any more stress to Sarah's life, by her feeling harassed by him.

Sarah couldn't quite work John out. He was very polite and very kind; except on their very first meeting when he had been very cocky. But she was always left with the feeling that there was something he wasn't saying. But today she had felt completely exhausted and drained by the whole Margaret situation and she just wanted to be left alone, and she was grateful that John had taken the hint.

She had not been taking any bookings for readings either for the next few days, after the police had told her it would take a couple of weeks for Margaret's body to be released. She was considering going away for at least a couple of days.

She had thought about doing that after Margaret was buried, but now that the police had given her the all clear for two weeks, it was tempting to go away before the funeral. She felt she could really do with a break.

"One major incident could throw your whole life completely upside down," she thought. John was pacing up and down in his parlour strategizing and rehearsing a speech when it dawned on him.

What did he know about Sarah? She was straight, uncomplicated in other words, no game playing, lying or manipulating. Actually, it was impossible to play games with her, she simply did not allow it. Not that she actually said so, "do not play games Mr O'Connor." It was her way of being that simply did not allow it. And that was one of the things that really attracted him to her.

There was no pretence with Sarah, just kind and gentle generosity. And if he hadn't also experienced her strength he would have said naïve. Non judge mental could be mistaken for naivety. She simply chose to see the goodness in people rather than the bad, which allowed people around her to rise to the occasion, so to speak.

"Wow, what a woman Sarah was, all class without any airs and graces." So John decided that he would call on her in a couple of days, giving her a chance to rest a bit on her own. And then simply say that he wanted to offer her a few days away, giving her a chance to put some distance between herself and the situation she found herself in, regarding Margaret's death and aftermath. And to offer it in such a way, that Sarah felt totally free to choose to take him up on his offer or not.

After all, she was the kind of woman you couldn't pressure into doing anything she didn't wish to do. And with that decision under his belt, he was actually able to get on with some work, and from time to time have some pleasant thoughts about Sarah.

After a couple of days just resting, walking and meditating, Sarah felt a lot better. But she was longing for some countryside. She loved the fresh air, the scenery and it didn't matter whether it was woods, mountains or sea. Just anything natural that made her feel closer to the spirit world. And the spirits were obviously listening because she had no more than thought the thought before the phone rang.

It was John who called and asked if he could call on her that day as he wanted to ask her something. She said yes, and an hour later he was knocking on her back door. John made it brief before he could lose his bottle, and invited her on a trip to the lakes. And who was she to argue with the spirits?

They ran the show in her world. John was surprised how easy it had been. He had told her that he needed a few days away, which was true, and that he thought she might too. And all Sarah had said was, "That sounds lovely, when were you thinking of going?"

"As soon as possible," John had said, "so we are back in time for the release of Margaret's body." John had then told her he would send a car for her the next day, and asked her if that was enough time for her to get ready. And Sarah had told him that was perfect, and they had agreed a time and John had left.

John had sat in his car for a long time after, amazed at how easy it had been. How come this very independent woman had so easily agreed to come away with him? She obviously trusted in something whether that be her own judgement or him or both, he wasn't sure. And quite frankly he didn't care!

This woman who had his heart and stomach do double flips every time he saw her or spoke to her, was coming to the lakes with him. He would have her all to himself for several days! John was stunned, excited and very nervous. John O'Connor was nervous to spend time alone with a woman, now that was a first!

Oh well, he kind of liked it, it made a change from his "normal" life. John had arranged for a taxi cab to pick Sarah up from her house, and to take her to an arranged meeting point outside of the city, where he would pick her up in one of his incognito cars, incognito to the mob that was.

31

He didn't want Sarah to get into any trouble of any kind because of any association with him. John was already waiting for her when she arrived in the taxi cab. He had actually been there for nearly half an hour when she arrived. He had allowed himself plenty of time because he didn't want anything to go wrong, as in Sarah arriving before him and wondering if she was in the right place.

He wanted her to feel relaxed, taken care of and happy in his company as a guest of his. When Sarah's taxi cab pulled up John almost swallowed his heart. He had to pull himself together, otherwise he might make her feel nervous too.

John rushed "calmly" out of the car and opened the cab door for her while asking the driver to put her luggage in the trunk of his car. John then escorted her to his waiting car, walking alongside her, using his arms to guide her towards the front passenger seat.

He had opted for driving himself for two reasons; one Sarah might have found having to sit in the back seat with him for such a fairly long journey a bit too intimate, so by him driving, he would have to concentrate on the road rather than "drooling" over her while pretending not to. And secondly, he wanted her all to himself without interruption or prying eyes.

When they were both seated in the car John asked Sarah if she was comfortable, or did she want to go to a diner to freshen up. A polite way of saying, "do you need the restroom?," he just wanted her to be as comfortable as possible the entire trip.

Sarah told him she was fine and asked how long the journey would take to the final destination.

"About two and a half hours," he told her. The experience of having her all to himself, next to him in the car, was almost overwhelming. He had never sat next to someone who felt so peaceful and yet there was a vulnerability about her that was extremely attractive. And it certainly brought out the best in him.

It brought out the caring, protective side on a level he was sure he had never felt before. She was so beautiful sitting there completely in her own world. There was something very childlike about her, an innocence that could only be described as divine. There was no judgment in her at all, only straight forward solutions, at least that was how he saw her.

She was like a breath of fresh air in his life which was full of polluted shitty people. And for now he was content just to have her next to him in his car, away from prying eyes and everyday life. They didn't exchange a single word for the rest of the journey and the peace he felt was having an enormous calming effect on him.

And he knew her well enough now to know that if she had needed anything, like the restroom or food or drink she would have told him so. He had given her a bottle of water at the start of their journey which she had been sipping on from time to time throughout.

They eventually reached their destination, John's cabin in the woods by Lake Oscaleta which was one of three lakes in the area of Westchester County, upstate New York. The cabin was situated in a beautiful corner, up against a large rock with woodland around it, and a path leading down to a long wooden jetty. But no boat, as John was not a boat man.

The place was full of light and magic but very well hidden from view if you didn't know it was there. Sarah got out of the car slowly and just took in the sight and the fresh air. John watched her walk down to the jetty, she walked all the way out to the tip which ended in a t-shape, and just stood there taking it all in.

John left her to it, and took their bags out of the trunk and brought them inside the cabin. The bedrooms where on opposite sides of the living room so John hoped that Sarah would feel that she had as much privacy as she needed. All he wanted was for her to be relaxed and have a well-deserved rest.

The journey had been so peaceful, and she was so grateful that John had been silent all the way there. The scenery had been entertaining and varied, and her mind had had free reign to let go of the city and the last few day's events.

As John had stopped the car, she hadn't even noticed the cabin, all she had seen were the lake and the sun sparkling upon it. It was midday or thereabout as the sun was high in the sky. The lake had tiny little ripples on it, and the only sounds, was the sounds of the bird singing, flying high in the sky.

In a place like this, she felt so close to the divine and the spirit world. As Sarah stood there on the jetty, Margaret showed herself to her. Margaret was very calm and very clear in her communication. She told Sarah that she was fine and that she was very grateful for everything she had done for her, and was doing for her. And that she knew her boys were in safe hands.

She also told Sarah that John was safe under her protection as she, Sarah brought the divine light with her wherever she went, and that everything was going to be okay in the end. After that "appearance" Sarah was enjoying the peacefulness of the spirit world and the beauty of nature rolled into one. And the reassurance that gave her, living her life guided in the right direction always.

John was surprised by how peaceful he felt after having been in the car with Sarah for that amount of time. Not a word had been spoken and still such a peaceful space. Especially considering why they had been thrown together in the first place and which was one of the reasons they both needed a break, to get away from the whole sorry situation.

He had not unpacked a thing or started to organise any food. He had been standing by the window mesmerised by the figure down on the jetty by the lake. Sarah had been completely still for what seemed like an eternity and god only knew what was going through her mind.

This woman seemed to always be in a state of…Some kind of…He couldn't quite find the words. Grace? Peace? No it was more than that. And whatever it was, John liked it. He snapped out of his state of trance and started to organise things inside the cabin. And after having put Sarah's bags in the room she would be sleeping in, he even forgot about her for a while.

He just slipped into old habits of making himself comfortable in this, for him, a sacred space. He went up to the cabin alone as often as he could to get away from everything and everyone, under the disguise that he had business out of town that he had to take care of alone.

He didn't want anyone to know about his cabin apart from Oscar and Rose. He loved the place. No one to bother him about anything, he even enjoyed his own cooking and he was actually a very good cook. Not that he would ever tell Rose that, she was always worried about his food wellbeing when he went to the cabin.

Rose prided herself on her cooking and she always wanted to hear how lucky John was to have her to look after him. And granted, Rose was a great cook, but he would always be able to manage without her if he had to. He had made a light and fluffy vegetable omelette with golden brown toast, real butter and tea for lunch. And he was just about to call Sarah back from the lake when she walked through the door.

"I didn't realise how hungry I was until I smelt the cooking of food," Sarah said and went and sat down at the already set table outside on the veranda, in the most natural manner. John loved the way she so naturally fitted in, in any situation.

So far, it seemed that there was nothing she couldn't adjust to in seconds. They chatted away about everything and nothing, and when Sarah smiled or laughed her whole face lit up. And he could easily imagine her as a little girl, amazed by the wonders of the world.

He was sitting there and taking all of her in, as the happiest man in the world, when Sarah suddenly stopped, and for the first time looked a bit shy and uncomfortable and there was an awkward silence.

"Oh my god, she is human, after all," John thought, "And now I have embarrassed her."

"Mr O'Connor, why are you looking at me like that? Have I said something really silly?" The words came out of her mouth before she could stop and think, and she regretted it the minute she had said it.

John looked surprised at Sarah's reaction, and was about to respond to her when she got up and said, "Let me clear the table and do the dishes since you were kind enough to cook." John felt like a price idiot. While he had been sitting there soaking in her beauty, she had taken his expression the wrong way, obviously thinking that he was laughing at her.

"How could he put things right without giving himself away? This is a tricky one." Again, he couldn't believe how tough and confident John O'Connor, could be reduced to a pathetic teenager in the presence of a lady. And that was just it, she was a lady, and John wasn't used to ladies. Not for the last twenty years anyway.

There were a lot of ladies around when he was young; his mother's friends had all been ladies. And back then, he had not known anything else. For the last twenty years since his parents disappeared, he had mainly been surrounded by gold diggers, low life sluts and prostitutes.

Gold diggers who would do anything to get his attention and be part of his lifestyle, sluts who would sleep with you for a few decent meals and some jewellery and of course prostitutes who was trying to earn a living. That's why, he had lost respect for women and had treated them according to his opinion of them.

Then there was Sarah, she was something else, very different from the women he was surrounded by. Sarah was so natural, elegant and graceful, apart from that moment earlier by the table.

"What had really made her lose her countenance?" He would do everything in his power to put that right, to make her feel comfortable again.

Chapter Five

While Sarah was doing the dishes she was examining what had happened at the table. It wasn't like her to be faced by anyone in that manner, but the way John had looked at her had made her feel like a silly little girl.

John was probably used to very sophisticated ladies and she obviously came across as a bit childlike to him. Not that she very often behaved very childlike, but she had felt so good and relaxed in these beautiful and peaceful surroundings, that she had got a bit carried away. She must have come across as childish to him.

John's face had been one of amusement and she hadn't felt that silly in a very long time, and it had made her feel very uncomfortable. When she had finished the washing up, she found John still out on the veranda. John had heard the footsteps, and as she approached he turned towards her about to speak, anything to break the ice, but before he got a chance, Sarah spoke.

"Mr O'Connor, I am sorry I was so rude earlier, I don't know what came over me. I was so excited at being here in this beautiful place and found myself behaving very childlike, and I simply got embarrassed when I saw the look on your face. I felt that I had made a fool of myself. I am sure you are used to very sophisticated ladies, who would not bore you in such a manner."

Another factor was that Sarah felt, that John had all the power and that she was at his mercy. They were at his cabin, miles away from anyone she knew. She had not expected for them to be alone.

She had thought he would have brought Oscar and Rose along too. Even when it had been just the two of them in the car, she had thought that Oscar and Rose had probably gone ahead to prepare everything. So Sarah was also worried what John might think of her, a single woman travelling with a single very powerful man, who probably was used to getting what he wants.

She could not believe she had put herself in such a position without checking all the arrangements first, she had blindly trusted the spirits. Now she felt like a complete gullible fool, "What must he think of me?" She felt more and more mortified by the minute.

Oh my god what have I done, he can do anything to me and no one would ever know. He might be really worried about what I might know and this was an easy way to get rid of me. I must stay calm and trust that all will be well, which was the message from Margaret earlier.

When Sarah had finished her "speech," John really had to compose himself, to stop himself from rushing over to her, take her in his arms and reassure her that she could not be further from the truth.

Instead, he spoke in a friendly and mild manner and responded with, "Mrs Steel, please do not, in any way, feel embarrassed, for you have nothing to be embarrassed about. Believe me, I find your manner and your company very refreshing compared to what I am used to.

"In my business and the circles I move in, there are no sophisticated ladies, I can assure you. And I find your straightforwardness and honesty very welcoming, and I am pleased that you find this place pleasurable. Let's say no more about it, and please promise me that you will be yourself at all times.

"And if I, in any way, make you uncomfortable, please put me straight immediately. I am a big boy, I can take it," he said the last sentence with a cheeky grin on his face, hoping that would put her more at ease.

"Thank you Mr O'Connor, you are so kind," Sarah replied.

"Mrs Steel, please call me John, at least while we are up here," John requested.

"Okay John, in which case I have to insist on you calling me Sarah," was her reply.

"Of course, if you wish," John said and then asked, "Would you like to go for a walk Sarah?"

"Yes I would love that," Sarah replied. But inside, she was worried that going for a walk was code for, "I am going to bump you off, where no one will ever find you." As they were walking along the shore of the lake which was mainly wood land with small clearings now and then, they were both wrapped up in their own thoughts.

John was again thinking how Sarah kept on amazing him with her honesty and vulnerability, which in her came across as strength. He could no longer imagine his life without her in it. Sarah was thinking, despite all her immediate worries, how grateful she was for this break from the city.

She loved nature and the scenery around the lake was breath taking. She was also wondering why John had asked her to come, if it wasn't to bump her off. There must have been at least a dozen other people he could have taken.

She guessed he felt sorry for her, having to deal with Margaret's death and everything that needed to be organised around that. John really didn't come across as a gangster or a member of the mob. You normally had to be of Sicilian origin to be part of that world.

It was very hot and she wondered if the lake was safe to swim in. John must have read her thoughts, because the next thing she knew John said, "It's very hot, and if you like, we can go for a swim, but I suggest we do it at midnight when it's slightly cooler in the air and the water won't feel so cold. And it keeps you nice and cool for the rest of the night, making it easier to sleep."

She could relax for now, because if he was going to kill her, he would probably drown her in the lake! She had to laugh at herself, "This is going to be a great break, if all I am going to worry about is being bumped off by this handsome mobster!"

As they had been walking along the shore line, John had been wondering how he could suggest a swim that evening. He didn't want her to feel uneasy in any way in his company, let alone trusting his own reaction seeing her in a bathing suit. He didn't even know if she had brought one as he couldn't remember if he had told her she could swim in the lake.

He wasn't even sure if he had told her there was a lake, their conversation at the time had been so brief and the outcome so surprising. It wasn't that he desperately wanted or needed to see Sarah in a swimsuit, for now it was enough to be in her company.

More than anything, he was terrified of scaring her away. He also loved his midnight swim and did not want to exclude her. There was something magic about midnight when in good weather the moon was shining down on you.

"That sounds magical," Sarah said. Throughout her childhood her parents had taken her and her sister to the countryside where there were plenty of lakes, and her father had taught her and her sister to swim. She loved those deep lakes; there was something peaceful and powerful about them.

So she had packed a couple of bathing suits in case the opportunity should present itself.

"That's settled then," John said smiling to himself as yet again her natural openness and appreciation shone through. They got back to the cabin and Sarah decided to sit down on the jetty and read for a while. But mainly she wanted to stare out at the lake and the surrounding scenery.

Nature always had the same effect on her. It made her feel peaceful and divine, and most of all it really helped her to recharge her energy levels. John preferred to relax on the veranda and catching the views from there, and today the view had an extra bonus with the beautiful silhouette of Sarah sitting on the jetty. Neither of them seemed to be particularly hungry in the heat, just thirsty.

Sarah had taken a bottle of water with her with lovely cold water from the well by the cabin. She must have dozed off because she got woken up by someone stirring her gently, and for a moment she had no idea where she was, and she felt very drowsy from the heat, and she was so glad she had had the sense to wear a hat.

John had said Sarah's name very softly a couple of times before there was any reaction.

"Poor Sarah, she is exhausted," he thought. The last few days must really have taken their toll on her.

When Sarah finally opened her eyes and realised where she was and recognised John's face, she smiled shyly and said, "I must have dozed off."

He smiled back at her gently, helped her on her feet and said, "Dinner is ready, we will eat on the veranda in this glorious weather."

"Oh how lovely, I am starving," Sarah replied. His heart sang with joy at the way she had expressed herself, with excitement and appreciation.

"Do I have time to wash my hands before we eat?" She asked.

"Sure you do," John replied with a voice full of love and tenderness. She was still so full of appreciation and gratefulness for having been given this break from the city in this beautiful place; she didn't notice the change of tone in his voice.

Sarah had told everyone that she was going to visit her sister Anna, and she had told Anna not to mention to anyone that she had gone away with John O'Connor. They ate in silence. John had made a juicy fillet steak and salad with a nice tomato garnish and Sarah was devouring it all.

She had a very healthy appetite, one of the things John liked about her. He never grew tired of watching the way she loved and appreciated the good things in life. The things that mattered like peace, beauty, good food, generosity and kindness. And there was that childlike quality about her that had her be so natural about all of it.

After dinner, Sarah started to ask John questions about his family, where he grew up his parents and so on. John found it really hard to answer the questions. He didn't want to lie but he couldn't tell her the truth either. Not at this moment in time anyway, hopefully sometime in the future he would be able to.

So he told her that both his parents died when he was a teenager, and that he didn't really want to revisit that time, which was true. And that he had some distant relatives somewhere in the country, but that he had lost touch with them a long time ago.

All of it was true, but very sparse information. But luckily for now, Sarah seemed happy with what he had told her. So then it was his turn to hopefully find out a bit more about her background.

"How about you, do you have any family apart from you sister?" John asked.

"I have an aunt in New Jersey and a couple of cousins in New York."

"And your husband?" he asked regretting it the moment the question had passed his lips.

Sarah looked straight at him with sadness and regret in her eyes and said, "He died very young."

"I am sorry, I had no right to ask you that question."

Sarah looked straight at him again and said, "It's okay. It just brings back really sad memories." They fell silent for a little while and John couldn't bear the fact that he had caused her sadness, here of all places. This trip was supposed to give her some breathing space, not remind her of even more death.

"How could he have been so insensitive?" Sarah started to think back to when she first had met her husband. She had been so in love and he had been so handsome. She had only been fourteen and Charles (Charlie) had been sixteen.

Although it had all been very innocent, they had kept it a secret for a long time, because they were so young. In 1916, right in the middle of WW1, when Charlie had turned eighteen, he had felt it was his duty to go and fight, and so he did.

She had been worried sick the whole time he had been gone, but when he came back after the war they were more in love than ever and Charlie had asked Sarah's father permission to marry her as soon as possible.

Charlie's proposal had been magical. He had taken her back to the place where they had said goodbye before he went to war, got down on one knee and said, "The only thing that kept me going during the war, was the thought of coming back home to you. There were times that I wanted to give up and just

40

die, but then I would see your face and remember that I had promised you I would come back. Now, a life without you would be impossible, please say you will share your life with me."

Then he had pulled out the perfect ring in her eyes, one that she had seen in a shop window right there in New York before Charlie had left for Europe.

She must have looked like a question mark, when Charlie smiled and said, "I have been carrying this with me the entire time I was away, knowing that I had to bring it back to you. I knew you liked it, when we looked in that window that day we had been out shopping, before I left."

She had been so happy that he had come back alive and all she wanted was to share her life with him. She had been so worried that he would have changed beyond recognition, or didn't love her any more. But neither of those two fears had come to fruition, the nightmare had come later and very unexpectedly.

They had been so very happy, and had wanted to start a family, but Charlie was soon taken ill from having been gassed in the war. And in 1920, he had passed away at the age of twenty two. Sarah had been inconsolable for years after that.

Apart from the fact that she had lost Charlie, she was also devastated that they hadn't been able to conceive a child, so that she would have had some part of him left. She often even wished that they had made love before he went to war, when he would have been well enough to father a child.

Then her parents had died close together, and that had been the turning point for her finding her inner strength and appreciating all of life to the full. At the same time as Sarah was thinking about Charlie, John was wondering how he could ever compete with a, he assumed, beloved dead husband.

"I know I can be very insensitive sometimes, but I want you to know that I would never deliberately do or say anything to upset you. So please accept my apology, and please feel free to reprimand me if I ever step out of line again," John said breaking the silence at last.

Sarah smiled and said, "Don't be so hard on yourself, you have been nothing but kind to me. And thank you so much for yet another delicious meal, I think you might have missed your calling in life, you could have been a chef," Sarah said smiling again.

John laughed out loud, "Don't repeat that in company, I will lose my hard man image. No one even knows I can cook, let alone that I am good at it. If Rose, my housekeeper found out that she is not saving me from starvation, she would be very upset."

Sarah laughed and said, "Your secret is safe with me."

"Thank you," John said with a big grin on his face.

Chapter Six

For the rest of the evening, they just pottered around, clearing the table, washing the dishes and unpacking. John showed Sarah around the cabin starting with her bedroom and bathroom. She loved both, they were both in some ways very masculine but at the same time they had a feminine touch.

There were four bedrooms in total, one with an en suite which John had given to Sarah and another bathroom for the other three bedrooms to share. He had actually given Sarah his room, but of course he would not tell her that. He simply wanted Sarah to have the best of everything, he would sleep outside on the veranda if he had to, as long as Sarah was happy and comfortable.

She was like a precious goddess to him that he would protect and defend until his last breath. He knew that if he said that out loud, it would sound ridiculous, but it really was how he felt. At midnight, wrapped in towels they headed down to the jetty for their midnight swim.

John dropped his towel and jumped in first, to give Sarah some privacy by looking out on to the lake once he was in the water. Sarah followed but she used the ladder attached to the jetty to get into the water. The water felt slightly warm now that the air was cooler.

Sarah loved the water; it reminded her of her childhood, holidaying with her parents and sister. It was so peaceful doing it in the dark, something she had never done before. Not a sound apart from her strokes and the night birds.

She swam out away from the jetty for a few yards until she reached a point where it was no longer comfortable to go beyond, so she turned around and swam back to the jetty. And thanks to the ladder she could easily get out of the water by herself.

Back on the jetty, she wrapped herself in her towel, then turned and looked for John. John had meant to look out for Sarah, but had automatically slipped into his normal routine. He always swam as far as he could, which meant as far as he could go without being too exhausted to make it back.

He loved reaching far out on to the lake, it felt like the only place on the planet where no one could reach him, where he could finally have some peace. Then it suddenly hit him that he had completely abandoned Sarah, he turned around and swam as fast as he could back to shore and his jetty. There he found Sarah quite relaxed wrapped in her towel and smiling at him as he ascended the ladder.

"I am sorry I abandoned you like that. I am afraid I went into autopilot and completely forgot myself. I have never had a guest with me on my midnight swim before," John said apologetically as he dried himself off with his towel.

"I am glad you can go off and do what you would normally do up here, instead of feeling as if you have to take care of me all the time. After all, this is a break for you too, so I have decided that tomorrow, I will do all the cooking!" Sarah stated.

"Absolutely not! I love cooking. It really relaxes me, and this is the only place I get a chance to do so," John said quite determined.

"Have it your way, far from it, that I should be the one to take that pleasure away from you," Sarah said smiling from ear to ear in amusement.

"And I will be on washing up duty for the rest of our stay," she said equally as determined as John.

"Be my guest," John replied and it was his turn to smile from ear to ear. He had never liked washing up much. They sat for ages staring out on to the dark still lake. It was a full moon and the light sparkled like diamonds on the water.

"You are not scared of the dark or being alone, are you?" John asked Sarah, but it was more of a statement than a question.

"Not really," Sarah replied.

"I tend not to hang around areas that do not agree with me and if I absolutely have to, I ask the spirits to protect me." It was the first time she had spoken about that part of her life with him.

"I have spent most of my life in an area I'd rather not ever see again if I could," John blurted out and regretted it as soon as he had said it. He was now on dangerous ground and might be asked to explain himself which he was not prepared to do at this stage. Sarah turned her head abruptly after he had said it, with a look of huge surprise on her face.

"What on earth did he mean by that?" she asked herself.

"No offence Mr O'Connor, eh, I mean John, but you do not come across as a man who hates his neighbourhood, more as a man who owns the place and love the power that it gives him."

She had spoken very frankly and as soon as she had said it, she felt she had been a bit rude, considering she was a guest in his cabin.

To Sarah's surprised John just laughed and said, "Yes, life can be a bit deceiving sometimes, people are not always what they seem." There was a part of him that wanted her to know who he really was, not just the façade that most people saw.

"No you are right about that," Sarah said slipping into her own thoughts. She wanted to tell him what Margaret had told her the night that she died, but wasn't sure if that was a good idea just yet. They were both holding on to secrets they wished they could share with each other.

Sarah suddenly felt cold as a little shiver went through her body.

John noticed immediately and said, "Come on, let's go inside and put on some dry clothes and I shall light the fire."

It was amazing how cold it could get at night considering how hot it was during the day. They walked side by side back to the cabin and he would have loved to have put his arm around her to keep her warm and to feel her beautiful body next to him. But they weren't at this stage yet and they might never be, he thought with sadness.

After all, for Sarah this was just a "business" arrangement, which she probably wished she had never had to get involved with. She had not shown any signs that she really liked him in any way apart from as an acquaintance.

He felt that she treated him exactly the same way she would treat anyone else in the world. John sighed heavily at that thought, in fact he sighed so loudly that Sarah turned and looked at him questionably. And he just smiled back at her, trying to brush it off.

The next couple of days were fairly uneventful. They were similar to the first one, they had their meals on the veranda, they went for walks, then John would settle on the veranda and Sarah on the jetty and they would end each day with a midnight swim.

John wished they could stay there forever, just the two of them, never to return to the real world and all that was expected of him there. But after five days, he received a telegram from Oscar saying the police was ready to release Margaret's body.

Chapter Seven

John decided to tell Sarah about the telegram straight away, and at the same time give her the option of staying one more day, before they headed back to the city. After all, there was no rush. No one else was really bothered about Margaret, her body or her funeral, or so he thought…apart from Margaret's two boys of course, Sarah and himself.

John found Sarah in her usual place on the jetty. It had become her favourite place it seemed. She could sit there for hours just staring across the water. He knew because he had been watching her from the veranda. Although she always brought a book, she didn't seem to be reading much.

He would love to know what she was thinking in those long moments she was spending on her own. He would particularly like to know what she thought of him, if she thought of him at all. He felt a quick sharp pain in his heart at the thought of her not caring about him at all.

Even thinking that he was a jerk was better than indifference. "Pull yourself together." he thought to himself. There were a lot of stuff he would have to deal with when he got back to the city, and Sarah could not be too much of a distraction.

Even if he could get her interested in him, how could it ever work? Her life could possibly be in constant danger being associated with him. He would rather be without her than put her in any danger. Now, who was he kidding? He wanted her so badly that he felt he couldn't breathe sometimes.

Well, for now he would have to settle for one more day alone with her. John made his way down to the jetty, hoping and praying that she would like to stay another day. Sarah was sitting with her arms wrapped around her bended knees, her chin resting on the top of her knees staring out on to the lake.

John didn't really want to disturb her, she looked so peaceful. And the energy emanating from her was entering him as a calm wave of peace and tranquillity that he had never felt before, ever. He could lose himself in this woman forever, and never ever look back on his previous life. She really was all he needed; he could take her away from New York and start anew somewhere far away.

"Sarah," John said gently.

"Yeah?" Sarah replied without moving at all.

"The police are ready to release Margaret's body, so we can now start to make arrangements for the funeral."

Sarah turned her head sharpish and said, "Really? So soon?" and for a moment she looked disappointed.

Then she pulled herself together and said, "Okay, how soon do you want us to leave?" John was relieved to see that she didn't seem very eager to leave either.

"There is no hurry, we can stay another day if you wish," he said as kindly and relaxed as he could. He wanted it to be Sarah's choice.

"Oh god I don't really want to go back to the city yet, it is so lovely and peaceful here," she said with a plea in her eyes.

"Tomorrow it is then," John said quietly singing inside with joy at the thought of another day with her.

"I could stay here forever," Sarah said and stretched out on the jetty putting her hands behind her head and looking up to the sky.

She had said it as if no one could hear her, and when she realised what she had done, she looked at John with a shy smile and said, "Did I say that out loud?"

John had to stop himself from laughing out loud, as he didn't want to embarrass her again, but he was grinning from ear to ear when he said, "I know exactly how you feel."

"Yes but it's not real life is it?" Sarah said and looked really sad. It was the second time he had seen her like that, the first time had been when he had asked her about her late husband.

"Well, let's make the most of the time we have left here. What would you like to do for the rest of the day?" he asked. Sarah thought about it for a very long time before she answered.

"I would like to take a walk to the other side of the lake, so I can see all of this, (she gestured with her arm to the jetty, the cabin and the surroundings) from a distance. That way, I will have a memory of the whole picture rather than individual snapshots of each bit," she answered.

"Very well, but let's have lunch first and wait for the sun to cool off a little bit," John replied to her request. "Okay that sounds good," she said and got on her feet.

"And maybe we could have dinner on the jetty tonight?" She said half as a question half as a plea.

"I will carry the table and the chairs and set it all up," she added.

"No, you will not," John said almost horrified.

"But if the lady wants dinner on the jetty, the lady shall have dinner on the jetty, but I will organise it." He was so adamant that she decided she was not going to argue with him.

"Okay, but please let me know what I can do," Sarah said.

"Just turn up on time and promise to enjoy yourself," John replied.

"Oh that is a promise," Sarah said smiling.

John grinned and said, "You got yourself a date lady." And for a split second Sarah blushed and looked very shy.

And immediately John thought, "Oh no, I have embarrassed her again."

"I am very grateful; I hope I haven't asked for too much?" She asked looking slightly uncomfortable.

"Not at all," John said, "I shall enjoy it very much too. And I want to find out what the magic is with this jetty."

"Oh that, I don't think I can explain," Sarah replied.

"Just try," John asked, "I would love to know."

"Okay," Sarah said going into thinking mode. As John walked off to start arranging lunch, Sarah was left to her own thoughts again. She felt a little bit embarrassed that she had asked for dinner on the jetty.

She realised it took a lot of organising and she had not thought it through before she had opened her mouth, she had just got so carried away with making the most of her last day, with no thought for John at all. And he had refused to let her help too, which made it even worse.

For a while now, she had actually considered moving out of the city to a nice country life somewhere. And John's place was beautiful and she knew she would probably never come here again. Once Margaret's funeral was over, John and she would go their separate ways to their very different lives.

Not that she minded that, she had no place in his world. She would never want to be associated with his world in the city after this. But for the last few days, she had completely forgotten about her life in the city, and just been in the moment without a thought about tomorrow at all.

She now felt very guilty that John probably had felt obliged to accept her request. But later that afternoon, after their walk, as John started to carry things down to the jetty, he was whistling away and looked as happy as Larry. This made her relaxed, as he obviously was enjoying himself.

Maybe he was looking forward to it as much as she did? They had, for the most part, got on really well, despite their very different lifestyles and view of life in the city. It was probably because they were on neutral ground and they both just wanted to enjoy themselves and relax, on a well-earned break.

Somehow the "real" world did not exist at the cabin. They had lovely homemade burgers in a bun on the veranda for lunch with fresh salad, before they went for their walk. They were on the sunny north side of the lake and you couldn't walk around the entire lake so he took her through some paths he knew on the east side where they could get to a point where they could see some of his property.

You could hardly see his cabin from the other shore as it nicely blended into the scenery, and Sarah felt that maybe that was the idea. She had the distinct feeling that John O'Connor was a very private man, apart from his outwardly city gangster "image."

The idea was kind of a contradiction in itself, but still that was the feeling she got about John. She felt that sometimes the whole persona was just a façade. But a façade for what, that was the question she didn't know the answer to.

John had wanted to get some idea of what kind of funeral Sarah wanted for Margaret, but he didn't want to ask while they were still in the beautiful setting of the cabin, that she seemed to love as much as he did. Their walk lasted a good couple of hours and they had stopped many times to take in the different views of the lake as they walked along.

She had been really surprised by how hard it was to spot his cabin from the other shore and John was very glad that someone who had spent quite a few days at his cabin found it hard to spot. After all, that was his intention, to be secluded and private. He really loved the place, every bit of it.

The dinner that night on the jetty was magical for both of them, but for very different reasons. For John, it was being with Sarah in her favourite place and giving her what she wanted the most at that moment, and he got to share it with her. She started to tell him about why she would sit there for hours staring into space.

She told him that out there, in nature, with none or very little noise and distractions, she could link with spirits very easily. She could "speak" to a group of them at the same time, and she would ask them questions and they would offer her a lot of information. And when she went to bed, she would write down what she wanted to remember.

She told him that the spirits always felt closer to her when she was out in nature, it was as if there were no barriers, in comparison to the city, where she would get interrupted by lots of different noises all the time.

Sarah was so alive and excited when she spoke about it; it was obvious that it was her passion. And she spoke of it in such a natural manner, as if it was the most "normal" thing in the world. John took it all in, Sarah's passion, how she came alive when she talked about it and of course, her beauty. This was who she really was, this was the real Sarah and he loved it, all of it!

He had never really thought about spirits before, an afterlife or anything like that. But Sarah made it sound like the most real and natural thing in the world. And listening to her, he felt that it must be the way she explained it all, because he believed her. She was not mad in anyway, that he was absolutely sure of.

Did this mean that his parents were watching over him? He wanted to ask if Margaret had been in touch, but at the same time, he wanted to leave that subject well alone for two reasons. One, he didn't want to break the spell of the evening, and two, Sarah might then have questions for him that he wasn't prepared to answer.

Not because he particularly felt he needed to keep anything from her any more, at this point, he would happily tell her his whole life story, but he did not want to put her in any danger. The less she knew, the safer she would be. He realised that he had drifted off, when he heard her say, "John, are you listening to me?"

"Oh sorry, I was listening and then I started thinking about if my parents can see me?" he replied. Sarah smiled, a soft and compassionate smile as to say, I know how you feel.

And then she said, "I am sure they are watching over you all the time, keeping you safe."

"Have they been in touch with you?" he asked. And the minute he had asked the question, he was stunned that such a question would ever cross his lips.

"I have spoken to them briefly," Sarah replied. Well, now he really was stunned.

"Really? When? What did they say?" John asked bewildered. Her smile was so gentle that he felt sixteen again and he just wanted to cry. He was working really hard not to completely fall apart in front of her.

"John, they love you very much, and they are always watching over you. Their job is to keep you safe, and as far as I can see, they are doing a good job. They didn't get into details to keep me safe," she finished.

Now, he was even more stunned. This woman never stopped surprising him. "Were his parents actually communicating with her?"

He felt totally confused and as if the wind had been knocked out of him. He wasn't sure whether it was the sun earlier that day, the food or the wine, but suddenly he felt very light headed and very vulnerable. He had not cried since his parents disappeared twenty years ago. But after that conversation, John started to sob, and kept on sobbing for how long he didn't know.

All he remembered was that Sarah came over to him and gently pulled him to his feet and led him to his room and gently helped him to lie down on his bed and took off his shoes. Then she held his hand and stroked his head for what seemed to be hours, until he finally fell asleep.

Sarah had really enjoyed the dinner on the jetty and the food had been great. Fresh grilled salmon, with lovely oriental seasoning and mashed potatoes and lightly roasted vegetables.

John had asked her about what was going on in her mind while she spent hours on the jetty staring into space. And for once, she didn't feel uncomfortable being asked about her profession. Not only that, she felt heard and understood.

Her parents had never understood but they had accepted it. When John had asked about his parents, she really got how much he missed them, and how devastated he had been when they died. Deep down, John was such a good man and she wondered how he had got into the "messy" business he was in.

She knew that underneath the tough guy exterior, there was a very kind and gentle man. She was guessing that when his parents died, he developed this hard exterior to make sure he was safe and protected from the tough world out there. She had watched him sob and fall apart for quite some time before she decided to go over and comfort him.

She knew it was a big deal for John to break down in front of her, and that in that moment, he had no choice. His body and soul wanted to let go and release the pain and grief he had held on to for so long. She was sure that by the time she had led him away from the jetty, John was no longer present to his surroundings, only his inner pain.

Sarah had sat with him for nearly two hours after getting him into bed, holding his hand and stroking his hair as you would a child, until he was sleeping peacefully.

Chapter Eight

When John woke up the next morning, his body felt very heavy. But he also felt very peaceful as if a dark cloud had lifted from his mind and body. It took him a few minutes to remember where he was and what had happened. But before all of that, in that first moment when he had opened his eyes, there had been blissful nothingness.

The most wonderful feeling he could ever remember having. Then slowly it all started to come back to him. The dinner, the conversation, Sarah's beautiful face and the painful moment when he got present to again, after twenty years, the devastating pain of losing his parents.

There was a part of him that felt deeply ashamed of having broken down in front of Sarah, but he also knew that nothing could have prevented that from happen the night before. He had reached a point of no return, with his memories that he had kept pent up for twenty years.

When they had spoken the night before, Sarah's presence had made it possible for him to let go and release it all. It was the look on her face of compassion, understanding and empathy that had done it, someone who understood his pain and despair and who was on his side. Someone who did not judge him.

The problem he now faced, was how could he ever go back to being the in-control gangster, John O'Connor with Sarah? Now that she had seen the most vulnerable side of him. On the other hand, he felt relieved that there was one person in the world that he could actually fully be himself with.

He was now stripped "naked" in front of her and maybe, just maybe that could be a good thing. He got up put his dressing gown on, and headed for the living room, and was very surprised to find Sarah asleep on the sofa.

She looked so peaceful he didn't want to wake her, so he quietly headed back through the hallway to the bathroom and had a shower, washing the last pieces of painful emotions away.

Sarah was still asleep when he looked in on her on his way back from the bathroom. "She must be exhausted," he thought. And slowly the memories came back to him of Sarah holding his hand and stroking his hair. God knows what time she got to sleep. What had he done to deserve this beautiful inside and out angel coming into his life?

He got dressed and went to the kitchen, which was on his side of the cabin, and made some fresh coffee. He then poured it into two cups and brought them into the living room. He sat down opposite her on the other sofa, sipping his coffee, watching her sleep.

He had drifted off into deep thoughts when he heard a very soft, "Good morning," from Sarah.

"Good morning," he answered back and asked, "How are you feeling?"

"It should be me asking you that," she replied with a very gentle smile on her face.

"Oh the storm is over, and I feel very peaceful thanks to you," John answered, feeling very relaxed and not at all awkward.

"I'm glad, that was a long time coming, wasn't it?" Sarah said more as a statement than a question.

"Yes it was, and I am glad it was you who was there, when it did come. As a matter of fact I don't think anyone else could have got me there if I'm honest. So thank you. I think you might be my guardian angel," John said with a very earnest look on his face.

"Oh I'm not sure about that, I think your parents were given that job, don't you?" she asked with just as much earnest.

"Well you might be right, but whichever way it is, I'm sure glad that our paths crossed. Although it hasn't been under the best of circumstances," John said.

"Yes, me too John, me too, but under other circumstances we would probably never have met," Sarah replied. And there it was again, that stab in his heart region when she said his name in her soft and gentle manner.

And the wonderful thing was that he no longer felt he had to prove himself to her, strange really, after he had behaved like a baby the night before. But somehow he felt that he had impressed her more than any tough guy routine he could have pulled on her. This was a strange new world to John.

"May I ask why you slept on the sofa last night?" John asked.

"You took a very long time to settle down after your release of emotions and I wanted to be nearby so that I could hear you if you woke up in distress, which can happen after an episode like that. Believe me, I have been there myself after my husband and my parents died," Sarah answered.

Sarah chose her words very carefully, because she felt this was a delicate matter for a "tough" guy like John.

"Thank you," he said and looked her straight in the eyes.

"I reckon I am indebted to you for the rest of my life," John said it with warmth, appreciation and humour. And he really meant it in two ways; one because he felt exactly like that, that she had somehow saved his life. And secondly he now had a very good excuse for keeping her in his life forever, or so he thought anyway.

"You might have to return the favour one day," the words were out of her mouth before she could stop herself. She wasn't serious; it was just something you said to make the other person feel a bit better about the "favour". John looked really surprised, but also amused in a kind way.

"Lady, eh Sarah, you can cry on my shoulder any time," he said and could feel a little bit of that old cocky John O'Connor persona coming through. Wow, that character had really become who he was over the years. Frightening really, especially if he was no longer able to control it in Sarah's company.

He immediately corrected himself and said, "I didn't mean to sound so cocky. I did mean it though, that anytime you need someone for anything however small, I'm your man."

Sarah smiled gently and said, "Thank you John, I think I already know that. And thank you for saying it. What time will we be leaving?" she then asked.

"Is 6 o'clock too late for you? That way we can make the most of the day, before leaving," John replied.

"Sounds good, because that means I get a few more hours here," Sarah said with contentment.

"Yes you do, so that's settled then. I shall get everything ready for departure," John said heading for the kitchen.

"I will help you, and I shall start with clearing the table from last night. The flies and other insects has probably had a field day," she said as she got up and went to freshen up a little bit before taking on her task.

"No it's all under control, go and speak to your spirits, I want to know what they have to say for themselves," John said in good humour.

"Are you teasing me, Mr O'Connor," she said smiling and added in a teasing voice, "I can do that while I'm clearing the table. You do know we women can multi-task, don't you?"

"No I am serious, I really do want to know what they are telling you," John replied, looking scolded as a school boy and added, "Well, we might not get away at 6 o'clock then you know," grinning from ear to ear.

He had found out the night before, that when she connected with spirit, often hours went by and she didn't really notice because she had said time just seemed to stand still, when she was in that state of connection.

"I don't care though, I would be happy to stay up here forever to be honest." He suddenly felt a freedom to be completely honest with her about almost anything, apart from anything that could put her in danger.

"That's fine with me too, but unfortunately, we both have to make a living, and we do have a funeral to arrange," Sarah replied.

"Oh yes there is that I suppose," he said and grinned. She was right about the funeral of course, but not about having to make a living. He had enough money stashed away to last him for the rest of his life, both thanks to his parents who had made sure he was provided for before they died, and his dealings as a mob member.

He felt a lightness and happiness that he could not remember having felt before at least, not since his parents died. But how would that fit in with going back to the city he did not know.

He didn't really have much to do as he had people who came and cleaned and tidied the cabin for him and looked after it when he wasn't there. But he wanted Sarah to think he was busy so she felt free to enjoy herself without feeling that she had to keep him company.

He also wanted to go for a walk in the woods behind the cabin and he wanted to go by himself. There was a route he always took which relaxed him and gave him time to think. After Sarah had cleared the table and done the dishes and John had moved the table and chairs back on the veranda, Sarah had a shower, packed her bags and headed down to the jetty.

John made sure Sarah was well-settled down there and then went for his walk. He knew she wouldn't miss him for an hour or two, and he would only be about forty five minutes or so. This walk had always made him feel peaceful, and today was the same but with one difference.

He felt a heightened awareness, as if he saw everything clearer and the colours seemed brighter. The grass and the trees were so green, or maybe he just had never noticed before. It did feel as if his senses had been sharpened. And as he came to the familiar clearing in the woods, he could have sworn that for a split second, he saw his parents standing at the end of it.

They were smiling and looked really pleased to see him, and he felt this overwhelming sense of love wash over him. He smiled back at them, but before he could do anything else, they were gone. It was all over in a split second, and it could just be his imagination.

Anyway, to him it felt as if they were close by, watching over him. This to him meant, that all the hard work he had been doing over the years had been worthwhile, although it wasn't the kind of life he had wanted for himself before his parents died.

He lay down on the grass for a little while, staring up at the blue sky with his hands behind his head and his legs crossed. These for John, were the moments in life that made a huge difference to being able to carry on, pure peace and quiet.

Then suddenly, he "heard" his mother's voice, "You are on the right track John, just keep going and "listen" out for our guidance."

"Yes mum, I will thank you. I love you mum."

"I love you too, son." What the hell had happened to him? Had Sarah messed with his head? Trying to rationalise the whole thing he said to himself, "I must have been dreaming, and if not, no one knows if I thought I had spoken to my mum."

Even if it only was his own imagination, and in this moment in time, he didn't care. After what felt like an eternity, he got up and started walking back to the cabin, and when he looked at his watch, he realised that he had been gone a couple of hours. He sped up his walk back to the cabin hoping Sarah hadn't noticed.

As he turned the corner of the cabin and could see the jetty, he saw that Sarah was no longer there.

"Oh shit," he thought, "I hope she's not worried." And he now wished he had told her that he was going for a walk.

"John, I'm here," he heard her saying. She was sitting on the veranda. He was trying to suss out her mood although she seemed fine.

"Do you have any secrets I should know about?" Sarah asked with a huge, almost wicked, grin on her face. He knew she was only joking and that she was absolutely fine.

"I felt your energy leaving, so after a while, I decided to come up to the cabin and keep an eye on things, just in case," she said.

"Well, you are not the only one who has a "magic" place, you know," John replied with a 'so there' look on his face. Sarah started laughing, really laughing.

"Oh John, you are a very funny man, and you are entitled to your own space up here without me for sure. You do not need my permission," she was laughing as she said it.

"Fine, I shall not tell you what happened to me in the woods then," he replied grinning. And that remark had Sarah in stitches, as he had said it as if he was an important little boy. And Sarah's laughter was contagious and soon they were both in stitches.

They were laughing for ages and they both had tears streaming down their faces, almost unable to stop.

When they both had finally calmed down, John was standing there just smiling at Sarah and said, "I cannot remember the last time I laughed like that. Thank you for making these last few days very special."

"Thank you, for inviting me along, I have had a wonderful time," Sarah responded.

"How do you fancy a walk and a picnic?" John asked. It was a spur of the moment idea; he decided he wanted to show her his walk and the beautiful clearing it led to. And they could have a picnic on the clearing.

"That's sounds wonderful, I would love to," Sarah replied.

Chapter Nine

After Sarah had been sitting on the jetty for a while, she felt that John's energy had left the immediate cabin area. She had looked up towards the cabin and it had just seemed so quiet. Over the last few days, when she had been on the jetty, John had often been out of sight, but she had still "felt" his energy around.

This time, she couldn't feel his energy and knew that he definitely was not anywhere near the cabin. And for a split second, she had considered whether she should be worried or not, but she didn't sense that there was anything wrong. So she had settled down again, but after a while her mind started to play games with her.

"Where had he gone? Why hadn't he told her he was disappearing for a while?" Then she came to her senses and realised that he knew she would be at least a couple of hours on the jetty. And she also realised that he had not had any private time at all, while they had been at the cabin. And she hadn't once asked him if there was anything he wanted to do, or anything he would have liked to have done alone.

"Oh god, I have been so selfish and just soaked up the time and beauty of this place with no thought for him at all." She felt ashamed and embarrassed when she realised all of that. John had been so generous with her, a perfect host who had given her lots of options to choose from, making sure all her needs and "demands" had been taken care of.

There were probably lots of things John would do when he was at his cabin that he had not been able to do this time because of her. So he was probably now grabbing this last chance to do something he wanted to do, and whatever that was, it was none of her business.

Sarah insisted on preparing the picnic basket, and John happily let her. And he insisted on carrying everything, even with all of Sarah's objections. He would never let a woman carry anything heavy or awkward, especially not Sarah. So Sarah had to give in, in the end, because John was so insistent.

The wood was delightful and cooling, the birds where singing and the squirrels were running up and down the tree trunks keeping themselves busy. There was a variety of trees in these woods in upstate New York, beech, red oak, aspen, red maple, ash and sweet birch among some of them.

They walked in silence; John excited as a child that Sarah was there with him. Sarah, soaking in the atmosphere and beauty, very much in her own world. She always favoured water over trees, but the variety of trees made the walk so very interesting, and the soft earthy path was very gentle on her feet.

It was so very peaceful; it felt as if a tremendous calm had descended upon them. John was walking in front, showing the way and every so often he turned around to make sure Sarah was okay. Also catching a glimpse of her facial expression, he could tell that she loved it.

Her beautiful childlike wonder was taking it all in, which made him smile at the thought of how easy it was to please this woman in these surroundings. She obviously loved everything about nature; he had never seen anyone appreciate it as much as Sarah.

It was as if she became one with it all. He always felt amazing in her company, and he hardly noticed that he was carrying anything. Whatever happened when they got back to the city, he would be able to look back and remember this walk and all the other beautiful moments during their trip.

"Thank you for sharing this with me, I really appreciate it. I'm taking some lovely memories of the last few days back home with me," Sarah said breaking the silence. Her voice brought him back from his thoughts. Sarah thanking him felt strange, because for him the pleasure was all his.

"Believe me Sarah, the pleasure is all mine. As it is so wonderful to have someone here, who appreciate and take as much pleasure in this place as I do."

She smiled gently and said, "I know what you mean and I'm really glad that these last few days has been good for you too, as I was beginning to feel that I had taken great advantage of you while we have been here."

"You mustn't think that for a moment, I am not a person you can easily take advantage of Sarah." She had no idea how good the last few days had been for him, if she had, she might have run a mile. He wasn't exactly her type, he thought, not necessarily in looks but as in profession and life style.

Apart from the cabin, of course, which for her was probably the only acceptable thing about him. Her dead husband had probably been the most wonderful man, a war hero. And maybe no man could ever take his place. But if he ever got a chance, he would do everything in his power to give her a happy and comfortable life.

Comfort and material things he knew he could give her, love too. He felt so much love for her that it often overwhelmed him, but emotionally was he strong enough and sensitive enough for her? If he ever got to be her man, he did not want her to feel that she had to be the strong one emotionally.

He saw it as the man's job to protect the woman in every way, and he hadn't always done that. Truthfully, he had been a bit of a bastard from time to time. But in his defence, he had to say, that the women he had been associated with, did not exactly bring out the best in him. Money-grabbing, low-life, gold-diggers or prostitutes most of them.

Knowing what he knew now, he probably would have got as far away from the city as he possibly could have managed when his parents died. But instead he had wanted revenge, he had wanted to "put things right". And look where that had got him so far, a lonely, emotionally closed down, angry, calculating thirty six year old man. Or at least emotionally closed down, until the night before.

All he could do right now, was to enjoy the moment and have a memorable afternoon with Sarah in these beautiful surroundings. While all these thoughts were going on in his head, they had arrived at the clearing, and he realised that Sarah was standing beside him studying him, because he had stopped, but his thoughts had not. And he had no idea how long they had been standing there.

"Right, we have reached our destination," he said looking awkward.

"You were miles away," Sarah commented.

"Yes I guess I was. Never mind I'm back now," he said trying to avoid the subject.

"Where would you like to sit?" John asked her.

"By the stream would be nice," Sarah answered.

"The stream?" John asked looking like a big question mark looking around him to see if he could spot it.

"Yes, over there," she pointed to the far left hand corner of the clearing.

"Oh yes, of course," he said and started to walk in the direction she had pointed. Sarah walked behind John a little puzzled by his mood. When they reached the stream John put the picnic basket down and laid the blanket flat on the grass.

"Please," he said gesturing for her to sit down on the blanket. Sarah sat down and John was still standing, looking a bit lost and asked her.

"Are you hungry, would you like to eat straight away?"

"John sit down and relax for a moment," Sarah told him. And there it was again, that feeling he got when she said his name.

"Are you okay? You seem very absent-minded," Sarah's question jolted him back to the here and now.

"Yes I'm fine, I just got lost in thought on the walk here, preparing myself mentally for returning to the city, and making the most of the last few hours here in my sanctuary." He surprised himself how easily all of that had slipped off his tongue.

"Yes, I know what you mean," Sarah replied.

"I have been having similar thoughts myself. It is just so amazingly wonderful up here, I could probably stay here forever, but I guess the winters are not quite so friendly, which is a helpful thought," all of this more to herself than to him. And it was now Sarah's turn to stare into space, mentally being far away.

John smiled, "Well now that we have established that, let's have a wonderful afternoon. Okay?"

"Okay," Sarah replied and smiled too. They both lay down on the blanket and stared up into the sky, it was so blue it was hypnotising.

"I saw my parents here earlier," the words were out before he could stop himself.

"I know, they told me," Sarah shared with him. John sat up absolutely astonished at what Sarah had just said.

"Well there is no keeping secrets from you, is there?" He asked.

"Was it meant to be a secret? Is that why you took me here, not to tell me?" Sarah asked with both sweetness and tease in her voice.

"Now you are just annoying!" John said.

"I'm sorry," Sarah said but still with sweetness and tease in her voice, and a very cheeky look on her face. John was trying to be annoyed, but he couldn't, her approach was just so innocent.

She was teasing but she was not being nasty. Not that he could ever imagine her being nasty; he should just buy her a halo and put her on a pedestal and be done with it. Could anyone be as perfect as he made Sarah out to be? He was smiling at these ridiculous thoughts.

"What are you smiling at?" Sarah asked.

"Oh no, I have to have some secrets. So unless you can actually read my mind, I'm keeping this one to myself," John answered adamantly. There was no way he would let her know at this moment in time, how he really felt about her.

One, he wanted to delay the rejection, if that was what was coming. And secondly, that would make him look like a creep, who had got her up to the cabin under false pretences. He would rather keep her as a friend, than risking her running a million miles away from him. And it was all too complicated at the moment.

They had to deal with the funeral first of all, without anyone expecting that they had a friendship going. If they even had one after the funeral, Sarah might want to be left alone after that. Everything seemed so complicated, now that Sarah had entered his life. And at the same time, he wouldn't want it any other way.

"John, Jooooohn, hello anybody home?" Sarah called out.

"Oh sorry, I drifted again," John said apologetically.

"I know, I have been calling your name several times. Are you okay?" She asked.

"Yes I'm fine, just got a lot of things on my mind now that we are heading back."

"Yes I know, you said. Anything I can help you with?" she asked.

"No no, but thanks for asking," he replied.

"Okay, shall we eat then? Are you hungry?" Sarah asked.

"Yes starving, let's get this show on the road." He was finally back in reality and ready to have a great picnic. They ate all the food and chatted away swapping childhood stories, both in very high spirit.

Laughing at silly little things, and they both felt as if they didn't have a care in the world. Once they had eaten, they packed away the plates; cutlery and cups back in the basket, and lay down on the blanket side by side staring up at the sky again.

"Don't you think the sky is bluer here than in the city?" Sarah asked.

"Yes but then it would be, because there is no pollution getting in the way here," John explained.

"Yes, you are right of course," Sarah replied. Having full bellies and the afternoon sun on them, they both fell asleep for a while.

After a while, John began to stir as he felt someone very close to him, he had trained himself to sleep with one eye open so to speak, in case someone decided to attack him in the middle of the night. After all, it was a dangerous world he was operating in.

As a matter of fact, someone was leaning on his arm, so if this had been an attack, he would have been dead by now. Some "guard dog," he was! When he opened his eyes he saw and felt Sarah lying on his arm, on her side facing him. He laid very still not sure how to deal with the situation.

He didn't want to wake her, she looked so peaceful. And at the same time he didn't want her to think he was taking advantage of the situation. Sarah stirred slightly and he tried to wiggle away from her, but didn't quite manage to. So he decided to let her sleep and deal with the consequences later.

He laid back again relaxed listening to her breathing, and he felt so relaxed he fell asleep again. When he next woke up, Sarah was no longer resting on his arm; she wasn't even on the blanket. He sat up feeling a little bit of a panic, but then he saw her down by the stream.

She must have felt his gaze, because she turned around and waved. John waved back, got up and started walking in her direction, with a big smile on his face. She had taken her shoes off and was walking around in the water, cooling her feet down.

"I felt so hot when I woke up, as the sun was directly on us, so I decided to cool myself down this way. Do you want to join me?" Sarah asked invitingly. There was no suggestion from her that she knew she had slept on his arm. "Why not?" he thought, but only gave her a nod, sat down and took his shoes and socks off.

The water felt nice and cool on his hot feet. All the times he had done this walk by himself; he had never thought of doing this. He had only sat on the bank of the stream, he felt like such an amateur in nature compared to Sarah.

How many times had he felt really hot when he reached the clearing, and had sat in the shade to cool down before heading back to the cabin? What an idiot he was sometimes, but now it was time to stop beating himself up and be a man in front of this Goddess.

"This is fantastic, I wish I had thought of it," he said smiling at her. She turned around and smiled at him, and as she did she tripped on a stone and lost her balance. John was quick off the mark and grabbed her and pulled her close to make sure he kept his own balance.

She was so close; he could feel the top part of her body against his. She smelt so nice and her bosom felt incredibly arousing against his chest. He didn't want it to happen, but his body reacted to his arousal and he pulled away and steadied her quickly, for her not to feel his erection. And took charge of the situation by pulling back a bit and asked her if she was okay. Going into protective tough guy mode, helped his body to calm down.

"Yes I'm fine, thank you," Sarah answered.

"And your foot, any toes broken?" he asked.

"No I don't think so, I just lost my balance as I turned," Sarah replied. Her losing her balance happened so fast and before she knew it, she was in his arms. He felt so strong and safe, and it had been a long time since she had been in any ones arms. He was such a good man, why was he in the business he was in? Under different circumstances she could have possibly fallen for this man.

"Oh my god, what am I thinking?" Sarah asked herself. John had shown no signs of being interested in her, not once. But that wasn't quite true, was it? Now she was confused. He had offered her a lift that first night after her dinner with Margaret, and he had been quite cocky and full of himself too.

She had not taken much notice at all, because of who she believed him to be in the community. And after that she had been so consumed by Margaret's accident, her visit after and her death that she had only thought of him as a liaison with the funeral. And when he offered her this trip, she had only thought of herself, not if John might have had an ulterior motive.

There was also that afternoon on the veranda when John had looked at her strangely. At the time she had felt vulnerable and thought she had made a fool of herself, but looking back now, the look could have been interpreted in a different way too.

All these thoughts were racing through her mind, after she had noticed how he had pulled away from her as soon as he had steadied her from falling in the stream. This was awkward, and she now wondered what he thought of the fact that she had accepted his invitation to go away with him so easily.

Whatever was going on, John had been a perfect gentleman the whole trip. Sarah decided to put all these thoughts to one side and carry on being herself, and relate to him in the same way she had related to him before the "rescue hug".

"Let's get out of the water," John said taking her hand and helping her up on to the bank of the stream. He had no idea what was going through her mind, she had gone very quiet. They walked back to the blanket bare foot carrying their shoes in their hands.

The relaxed atmosphere between them had been broken, they both felt an attraction for the other, but didn't have a clue as to how the other one felt about them. They got back to the blanket and automatically started gathering up everything, both silent neither of them knowing what to say.

They walked in silence all the way back to the cabin, and when they had put everything down on the veranda, John said with more sharpness in his voice than he had intended,

"We will leave at 6 o'clock as planned, so we won't get back to the city too late. And I will call Oscar from a gas station when we get closer to let him know what time to book you a taxi cab for." And before Sarah had a chance to reply, John disappeared into the cabin.

"Okay," she said very quietly to herself.

"What had happened?" One accidental "hug" and John had gone ice-cold on her. The more she analysed it, she realised that John had been a perfect gentleman, friendly but kept a distance most of the time, apart from that night he had had his meltdown.

The sooner they got back to the city and got the funeral over and done with, the better, she thought. It was all getting very awkward, and she now really wished she had never accepted his invitation.

She went into the cabin and finished her packing, and at the same time trying to avoid John. When she was all done she called out to him wherever he might be, "I will be down at the jetty unless you need me for anything?"

As she walked through the living room, John popped his head round the door from the kitchen all smiles, "Okay, I don't need you for anything, so enjoy and I will come and get you when we are about to leave."

She had expected a stern looking John, and it completely threw her that he was all smiles. She could not work this man out, so she decided nor would she try to. John had seen the awkward look on Sarah's face as he answered her back.

"So, well done John, you have managed to do it again. Make her feel uncomfortable in your company. She is my guest here and I have handled lot of things very badly. How can I explain myself, unless I come clean about my feelings? And I can't do that, because that would put Sarah in a very awkward position. And me too."

"It would then seem as if I had only invited her to the cabin, to be close to her for my own benefits. And yes, that is partly true, but I had also wanted to give her a break from the stress of everything surrounding and including

Margaret's death. It is all such a mess and I now have to deal with the consequences of it all. But most of all I have to make things more comfortable between us, and I will do that right now. There is no time like the present," he thought.

He found Sarah in her favourite place down on the jetty, and he could sense that she wasn't her usual happy self. He sat down right next to her, having no idea what he was going to say. So he turned and looked her straight in the eyes to gain some courage.

Looking into those green eyes which were normally so kind, all he saw was sadness, shame and confusion. And in that moment, he decided to be honest and open, and just say it as it was.

"Dear Sarah, I'm sorry that I created this awkwardness between us earlier. I'm a man and you are a very beautiful woman, and being that close to you had my body react and I didn't want you to feel that, so I pulled away. And I also felt embarrassed, I didn't want you to think that I had invited you up here for any other reason than that I thought you could do with a break from it all.

"Maybe I should have brought Oscar and Rose, but I needed him to stay in town for me. And I also thought you would be more relaxed if there was only one stranger here, me, that is. So I apologise for not handling that incident very well, and I truly do not want there to be any awkwardness between us. Friends?"

"Friends," she said and they hugged each other without any awkwardness. It was just a lovely glorious hug between two friends. He was getting up to leave when Sarah grabbed his arm, wanting him to stay.

"Thank you for saying that and clearing the air. Because I had similar thoughts, worrying about what you thought of me coming up here on my own with you, a man I didn't know at all, but I was just so grateful for the offer, I couldn't say no, as I had already been planning to have a few days away in the country.

"So at the time, I didn't care how it might look from the outside, and the fact that I felt safe, and I knew the spirits would have warned me if I was in danger. And I must admit I didn't expect us to be alone on the trip.

"So thank you so very much for these beautiful days up here, they have done me the world of good. And I have very much enjoyed your company; you are a great man, very different from what I expected. Only god knows why you do what you do."

The last few words came out before she could stop herself, and she let out a small gasp before saying, "Oh John, I'm sorry I didn't mean to say that."

He smiled and took her hand and said, "Yes you did, and it's okay. I love your honesty, and maybe one day I will explain it to you."

And with that, he got up and said, "And now I must finish the last bit of packing." Sarah was so glad John had decided to clear the air. Now, she could enjoy the little time she had left down on the jetty, her favourite spot.

Soon enough, she would be back in reality and that didn't seem appealing any more. She had loved her life for a long time, the freedom of being single and her and clients. Never feeling that anything was missing, but now all of a sudden it felt like going home, was going to be lonely.

"What has come over me? A few days in the company of a handsome and nice man, and suddenly my life feels dull and boring. Hang on a minute; I have just admitted to myself that not only have I enjoyed John's company, but that I also find him attractive.

"Oh no, in a matter of a few days my whole world has been turned upside down, this is the last thing I need. My life has finally been calm and steady and I can please myself, I really don't need this. Especially with someone so not suited, in terms of our different lives, and I want nothing to do with his world!"

But what she did know was, that the spirits worked in mysterious ways and all she had to do, was trust the process, which sometimes was the hardest part. And she still always had a choice in which direction she went and at the moment she was conflicted.

Apart from all that, John had said that he didn't have an ulterior motive when inviting her up to the cabin. So did that mean he wasn't attracted to her and had never thought of her in that way? He had said that being that close to her had had him "react," but then again that was fairly natural for a man. He had also said she was a very beautiful woman.

"Oh god, I have to stop thinking about this now, or it will drive me crazy. Maybe I'm just missing a bit of male attention? I was fine before Margaret's accident and I will be fine again, after all this is over. Am I really attracted to him, or is he just the first man I have felt good around since Charlie died?"

Bottom line, they had had a good time, she felt rested and at least they felt comfortable in each other's company most of the time, which would make it easier to organise the funeral. She must have fallen asleep, because at 6 o'clock she was gently woken up by John.

"Time to head off, sleepy head," he said gently. She smiled and stretched and took one last look at the beautiful view, that she loved so much.

"Okay if we must," she said and sighed. At 6.30 pm, the car was packed and they were ready to set off.

As Sarah took one last look out on to the deep mysterious lake, the green lush trees both by the cabin and around the whole shoreline and the blue, blue sky she looked at John and said, "Thank you so much for sharing this beautiful space with me."

"It has been an absolute pleasure, and if you are lucky, I shall take you here again," John replied and winked at her with the good old John O'Connor charm. He now felt very comfortable and confident around her, as he no longer had anything to hide.

John noticed that Sarah blushed deeply as he winked at her, which really got him excited. Because he took it as a sign that she did like him, but not to embarrass her he didn't let on that he had seen it. He was just joyful inside that she had blushed, because to him it meant that she might just like him as a little bit more than a friend.

Sarah felt herself blush as John winked at her and she felt embarrassed. She was falling for him and she didn't want to. She wasn't sure if John had noticed; if he had he wasn't letting on, a real gentleman. It was the first time since the beginning of her courtship with her late husband; she had felt silly and awkward around a man. And she had first met her late husband eighteen years ago.

She was used to being strong and self-sufficient, and she felt very comfortable with that. Independence and freedom was what she was used to now, getting close to someone could end up in loss and pain as she knew so well. She was thinking of both Charlie and her parents, but then again that was living in the past, letting it dictate the future.

John was different from any man she had ever known. She couldn't quite put her finger on it, but he was. He was also very confident, and she liked that. He had that in common with Charlie, who had also been a very confident man.

Sadness fell over her, thinking about Charlie and the life they should have had together, and the life that Charlie never got to have. Another thing John and Charlie had in common was, they were both very caring or at least John had been towards her. And the way he spoke about Oscar and Rose, she could tell that he was very fond of them and would always look after them.

And from a person looking from the outside, it looked to her as a two way thing. They took care of him and he took care of them. She kind of gathered that Oscar and Rose had been like parents to John, ever since his birth parents had died. Part of her wished that Margaret had not been a client of hers, and that she had never gone to dinner with her that fatal night, then she would never have met John.

She had felt so strong and in charge of her life for so long, and that had been very comfortable. And now all of a sudden she didn't know what she wanted anymore, and it felt very uncomfortable. But one last glance at the scenery and she sighed and thought, "this part has been worth it."

"What was that for?" John asked and smiled at her.

"I am going to miss that view," she answered.

"Well you know what I said earlier," John said with his cheeky grin.

She smiled and said, "Thank you." But her face was saying, "We both know that is not going to happen."

"I will take you here again," he said with determination, as if he had read her thoughts.

"You are not going to give up on me, are you, Mrs Steel?" His question made her smile and the words that fell out of her mouth was, "I will never give up on you John O'Connor."

"I am glad to hear it, so then we agree on something and that's a good thing," he said and grinned from ear to ear.

"Someone has to save me from myself." She couldn't help but laugh; he was such a charming man, so boyish sometimes.

"Ah, finally I have made her laugh, that has made my day…that has," he whistled as he shut the trunk and made his way around the car to the driver's side. And Sarah was still laughing getting into the car too. All in all, it had been a good few days, he thought.

Sarah remembered how worried she had been the first day when she had had serious thoughts about how John probably was going to bump her off, and get rid of her body, in case she knew too much and could expose him. She was smiling now at the thought of those thoughts, as she had completely forgotten about it after the first day, because John had been very caring and considerate the entire time.

They were chatting all the way back to Sarah's drop off point, the time had flown by with only one restroom stop, where John had called Oscar to arrange a taxicab for Sarah. A very different journey atmospherically, to the one on the way up. They had chatted about their childhood again, but he had not specified where exactly he had grown up.

They had also spoken about the neighbourhood they now both lived in, although quite far apart. And Sarah had been so tempted to ask him about his "line of work," but could not bring herself to do it. She didn't want to change the mood.

She could ask the spirits, but it really wasn't any of her business. And it would also violate his privacy, as she was really clear that she could only look into someone's life psychically, with their permission. There was a real sense of sadness when they said their good byes, by her taxicab.

"It has been an absolute pleasure getting to know you Sarah," John said and gave her a big bear hug.

"Likewise Mr O'Connor, eh John," was all she could manage to say. She got into the taxicab and he stood by the side waving her off, with a big smile on his face. She waved back and mustered up a faint smile.

Oscar was waiting in the wings with a small very neutral car, and would follow Sarah's taxicab at a safe distance, to make sure she got home safely. When it came to Sarah's safety, John would not take any chances. There were a lot of people that didn't wish him or anyone close to him, well.

Chapter Ten

John was normally the happiest when he was on his own, but Sarah had left behind an emptiness he had not felt before. Not the same kind of emptiness he had felt when his parents had died, this was different.

It felt as if his life had reached a crossroad, and there were decisions he would finally have to make about his future. There was so much he hadn't told Sarah, and keeping her in his life, meant keeping her safe. This would not be a small task. Even as just friends, it would not be easy, as the mob wouldn't know the difference.

Maybe the best thing to do was to get the funeral out of the way, and then go their separate ways. He was so confused about where he stood with Sarah, and what to do for the best. This was a whole new chapter for him, and he decided to get the funeral out of the way, and then he could think more clearly. Then an idea came to him.

They could have a decent "fake" funeral in the neighbourhood, where most of the mob would come and check out who else was there and try to work out who didn't? And then Sarah, Margaret's boys and himself could have a real funeral in a small country church somewhere. That way the boys and Sarah would be kept out of harm's way.

"What a brilliant idea," he thought.

"You clever son of a bitch, she will love you forever." Sarah felt sad and lonely after leaving John behind at the pickup point. She had not thought she would want a man in her life again, as no one could replace her beloved Charlie. Or maybe she just hadn't found someone who could, not replace him because no one could, but maybe someone who was his equal, just different.

John was funny, charming, caring and considerate, and she was beginning to feel like a woman again, around him. How could she now go back to her empty house and be happy again?

"Damn you Margaret for dying on me and putting me in this position." At that moment, the spirits were smiling at her, so she knew they were up to something. When they arrived at her house, the taxicab driver helped her with her bags.

And when she went to pay him, he gave her a salute and told her, "It's all taken care of ma'am."

"Oh okay," she said slightly surprised, "Thank you very much."

"My pleasure ma'am," the driver said and drove off. She suddenly had this sneaky feeling that he wasn't a taxicab driver at all. A man of John's position could pretty much arrange anything in this city.

Oscar waited until he had seen Sarah safely inside her house, before he headed back to John's house. Sarah left all her bags in her hallway and headed for the kitchen, she needed a cup of herbal tea for company and hydration.

When she got to the kitchen, she had the sense that someone had been there in her absence. The larder door was slightly open and she always made sure it was closed shut. She went over and opened the door and saw there was fresh bread.

She then opened the refrigerator and found a bottle of milk, butter and a selection of cold cuts. She sat down on the floor and burst into tears. Oscar and his wife! She had forgotten that John had asked for a set of keys to her house, so that Oscar could keep an eye on her house while she and John were away.

It was such a long time since someone had taken care of her that she couldn't help but get emotional. She could get used to this, she thought.

"Sarah, what are you thinking, you are an independent woman, don't fall apart on me now!" She said to herself. She was giving herself a good talking to. It wasn't that big a deal, a little bit of kindness never killed anyone! And with that she made herself a sandwich. The ham was beautiful; it literally melted in her mouth. And the bread was so fresh it still felt warm.

"I bet Oscar's wife Rose made it this evening," she thought. And the butter and mustard just added that extra, perfect flavour, such a great combination. She had chosen to sit in one of the armchairs by the window, the one that John had sat in, the day after Margaret's death.

She was remembering that quick embrace they had had earlier that day, when John had rescued her from falling in the stream. The incident had been over so quickly, but still something had happened to her in that brief moment. She had felt like a woman again, not that she didn't feel like a woman, but the way a

73

woman only feels when she is held by a man. Being alone was not so appealing any more.

She let out a big sigh and pulled herself to her feet, she felt exhausted. She didn't understand why, as she had had a great break in the beautiful countryside. But she didn't want to think about why tonight, she just wanted her bed.

She couldn't even be bothered to go through her usual bedtime routine, she just brushed her teeth and went to bed. Her bed felt so good and her bed sheets were so soft and they smelt so fresh.

"Of course, John and his crew!" and that was her last thought before she fell asleep. She had a restless sleep where she was walking in the woods, looking for John. She kept seeing his face, but then he would disappear again.

In the end she was back in the clearing where they had had their picnic, and there she saw Margaret standing on the bank of the stream with her hands stretched out to the sides, smiling at her.

"Margaret, you are still alive?" she shouted. Then Margaret turned around and walked away, and Sarah woke up. She felt a hand touching hers, and she could have sworn there was someone there in the room with her, but when she switched the light on there was no one there.

Okay, so someone wanted to reach her from the other side maybe? She looked at her alarm clock, it was only 4.30 am.

It was 3 am and John had only just finished off all the business with his guys. Even just a few days away had business piling up, and it seemed nobody knew who had killed off Margaret.

The whole neighbourhood was lying low, very unusual. Normally, someone had seen something or knew what had happened, but not this time. He had not had time to think about Sarah at all, apart from when Oscar popped his head around the door and gave him the thumbs up about her getting home safely.

The taxicab driver had taken the scenic route so no one expected that they had come from the same direction as John. So John had got home sooner than Sarah and therefore was already in a meeting with his guys by the time Oscar showed his face.

John now really thought he could give up all of this, and disappear somewhere where no one could ever find him, most likely somewhere abroad. All he wanted was Sarah. He could create a life for himself anywhere, as long as she was with him.

The desire and drive for revenge had gone; he really couldn't care less any more. Even though he had sworn as a young man that the bastards who killed his parents were going to pay for the rest of their lives, he was going to make sure of it. And he had never thought he could feel like that.

Never! Now everything he did seemed, meaningless, he was even questioning why he had wanted to do it in the first place. But in all fairness, he had been sixteen at the time and absolutely devastated and very, very angry.

At the time, the thought of revenge had given him something to focus on, and had kept him sane. But would he give up all of this, if he couldn't have Sarah? Now that was a question to ponder on. After those few days at the cabin, he really felt as if life would be pointless without her.

Damn, life has suddenly become very complicated, and some would say he was mad for thinking like that. His life was such a huge complication anyway, so to add a dame into the mix, was no big deal. But that would be men who had very little regard for the women in their lives.

For him, Sarah was the whole deal, the only thing that really mattered. To walk away from his life would be such a big gamble and puzzle to put together, and to leave no traces. And the biggest thing was to keep Sarah safe in the process, if she would have him.

How he would get her to be with him was a whole different ballgame. And one he had never played before, especially with so much stacked against him. But he would find a way, he always did. At least he had everywhere else in his life.

When he finally went to bed, he fell into a very restless sleep, where he was running up and down hills with the whole mob in tow, guns in their hands. And he could hear Sarah calling his name and calling for help, he was desperate to get to her, but he couldn't find her.

When he eventually found her, she was in a lake, desperately trying to hold her head above water, very distressed.

He was calling out to her, "Hold on Sarah, I'm coming," but then he suddenly felt a bullet in his back and he fell face down.

And his last thought was, "It's over, I can't save her!" And in that exact moment he woke up and he was wet through, his heart was racing and he felt panicky.

His first thought was, "Is Sarah okay?" It was 4am, he got dressed, went out the back door, walked down the tunnel and out to a back street a couple of blocks away. Got into an anonymous car, drove to a street a block away from Sara's house and walked to her back door making sure he wasn't seen and let himself in.

He was quiet as a mouse; he was good at this kind of thing. He had often been in someone's house without them knowing. He found his way to Sarah's bedroom where luckily the door was slightly ajar.

"Oh good," he thought, "That makes it easier." Sarah seemed to be asleep as she was very still, and he went close enough to hear her breathe.

"Thank god," he wanted to let out a big sigh of relief, but knew he couldn't. It would frighten the life out of her. Then Sarah stirred and started to turn, and he stood absolutely still, holding his breath.

"She must not see me, she will think I am a crazy stalker," he thought while standing there. Sarah turned back again and he very quietly left her bedroom. He left the way he had entered through the backdoor and decided he would put one of his guys on guard to watch over her at all times.

It would have to be very discreet, so no one noticed, especially Sarah. As she would probably go mad if she found out. She was a very independent woman, who wanted nothing to do with his life at the best of times. And if she, in any way, thought she was in danger because of him, he would never see her again. He was sure of it.

"Oh god, his life had just got over complicated, everything was based on lies and deceit. Ever since he was sixteen, he had had this attitude that some people were undesirable and disposable. And if they should happen to get caught in the crossfire, so be it.

But Sarah was irreplaceable to him and probably to a lot of other people too. After Sarah had switched on the light, she felt very calm, like someone was looking over her. So she switched the light back off, and went back to sleep.

When John got back to the car, he took a little drive around the neighbourhood, and it was exceptionally quiet. His guys had told him that the mob seemed a bit nervous at the moment, and no one knew who had bumped Margaret off. And it was making everyone a little bit uneasy.

It was always that way when no one knew what was going on, which didn't happen very often. John had spoken to his guys about how they would organise the funeral. It would look like the "state" had organised it, so that he himself did not look involved.

He would not tell Sarah any of this; he would only consult her on what kind of funeral she wanted for Margaret. And arrange the real one exactly according to her instructions. And on the actual day he would have her picked up and taken to a small country church where they would have the real funeral with Margaret's body.

And everything would be arranged the way Sarah had instructed. And of course Margaret's boys would be there too. He was really pleased about the real funeral, as it meant that Sarah would not be connected to Margaret in any way as far as the mob was concerned. And no one would see Sarah's face at the fake funeral in town, which meant, it was easier to keep her safe.

He doubted very much that any of the mob, would remember the face of a woman Margaret had had dinner with the night she died. Sarah had not drawn attention to herself in any way, and most of the men there that night mainly mob members, were more interested in the women who wanted attention and who were an easy lay.

Sarah woke up really late the next morning, it was almost 11 am. She was quite shocked, as she was normally an early riser. But so many things had happened in such a short space of time, so many feelings that she had not had to deal with for a long time.

Feeling nervous around a man that she liked, and not knowing how he felt about her. Someone dying, even though she didn't know her very well, it still brought up feelings of previous deaths. It made her feel the loss of her husband and her parents again, although that had been different as Margaret had not been a close family member or friend.

It still brought up the painful memories of loss from the past, and the concerns she had been left with about Margaret's life. Sarah had known that Margaret was troubled, but not quite sure what exactly she had been involved in.

In the readings Sarah had given Margaret, the messages that had come through had been mixed and confusing. They had indicated that Margaret was in danger from all directions, and that made perfect sense now, after Margaret's confession to Sarah on that fatal night when she died.

Margaret had been an informer for both the police and the mob, and the police had started to put pressure on her to dig deeper, and that in itself was dangerous. If the mob found out that you were or had been betraying them, you were dead.

But one thing Margaret had said that night did not make sense. She had said that, "When it comes to John, don't judge him too harshly. He is not like all the rest of them, he is kind and generous, and so if you need anything when I'm gone, you must turn to him for help. But be discreet for your own safety, because anyone close to John is an enemy to the rest of the mob."

Sarah thought for a moment, "What had Margaret meant by close to John? Had Margaret meant herself or me? But Margaret couldn't possibly have known that she, Sarah, would get close to John, so she must have meant herself. Had Margaret had an affair with John?"

Sarah wasn't the jealous type, but the thought of Margaret and John together did feel painful. Did John know that Margaret had been a double agent? Margaret believed that it was John who had arranged her "accident" that night. And she had mumbled, "He must have changed his mind about our deal."

"What had Margaret meant by that?" Margaret had said that the car which hit her had actually driven up on to the sidewalk, and had hit her hard enough to kill her. It was all so confusing.

"What had Margaret meant when she said, he must have changed his mind? Changed his mind about what?" And it suddenly occurred to Sarah that in her absence, John's "people" had been the ones in communication with the police, regarding the release of Margaret's body or vice versa.

On one hand, Margaret had told her what a great guy John was, on the other hand, she had thought he had let her down. Which one was it? Who was John O'Connor, really? And how had he really found out that Margaret's body was ready for release?

He must have "friends" in the "right" places. Sarah got tired of trying to work it all out, so many things just didn't add up. When it came to her life the spirits would only give her information on a need to know basis, or moment by moment in certain situations. Maybe, none of this was any of her business, and she should stop trying to work it out. Or had she arranged with the police to leave a message at her house, and that a friend would collect it and pass it on?

She could no longer remember. She just felt exhausted, as if everything was a huge effort. Even getting dressed, felt like too much hard work. She had pretty much always known what she wanted, but now everything made her feel uncertain.

When the funeral was over, she should walk away from it all, including John, and get back to her normal life. With that thought in her head she went back to bed and back to sleep. All she wanted to do was sleep. When she next woke up, it was 7pm.

At first, she was a bit disorientated, she didn't know where she was, what time it was, and what she was meant to be doing. John had had one of his guys keeping an eye on Sarah's house all day, and the report came back that there had been no movement all day.

John was worried, why was Sarah hiding away in her house? He wasn't sure what to do.

"Oh god, it was very stressful being worried about another human being, to the extent he worried about Sarah's wellbeing," he thought. He knew that his guys knew that Sarah was a very special lady to him; he could see it in their eyes, their sympathy and their genuine concern. John was very good to his guys, and in return they were very loyal to him.

They all wanted what he wanted, which made them a united team, that's why no one could touch them.

"Is she sick, stressed and tired, what?" He really wanted to go over to her house, but could not find an excuse.

"When have I ever needed an excuse to do anything?" He had reminded himself again, why this was different. One, he could not put her at risk, two he could not let her know that she was under "surveillance," and he didn't want to scare her away.

He wanted her so badly, he could barely think of anything else. It had been okay while they were at the cabin, when he had known that she was always around somewhere, and she could not leave without him.

But now, he had no control over her movements, and he had no idea when he would see her again apart from at the funeral. Would he ever see her again after that? He let out a big sigh, "I have to pull myself together."

He had all but forgotten that he could contact her regarding funeral arrangements. But he knew that the police had her phone tapped, so he didn't want to call her regarding any funeral arrangement. He would send a "delivery van" over with a message. Then Sarah would have to come to the door, and he could find out in general terms how she was.

Rose came into the room and told John there was a phone call for him.

"Who is it?" John asked.

"I don't know, she didn't say," Rose replied.

"She, it's a woman?"

"Yes John, a woman, you have heard of those, haven't you?" Rose said and laughed.

"Ha, ha very funny, you do know I pay your wages don't you?" John replied.

"Oh dear, lost your sense of humour, you must be in love!" Rose said and winked at him. John went bright red and couldn't think of a reply.

"Oh my god, you are, aren't you?" Rose said dumbfounded.

"I'd never thought I'd see the day; she is a lucky lady; I hope she realises that!"

"This conversation never happened. Do you understand?" John said really sternly.

"I understand," Rose said and winked again.

And as she left the room she said, "Don't keep her waiting now." Rose did know the potential danger a lady friend could be in, being connected to John, but she kept it light-hearted to hopefully help him snap out of the stressed mood he was in. John had butterflies running amok in his stomach and he felt as if he had to go to the toilet.

"What did she want? Why was she calling? For god's sake, pull yourself together man!" He was at the phone now, and took a deep breath.

"John O'Connor," he said in a very business-like voice.

"John, it's Sarah." There it was again, a stab in his chest whenever she said his name.

"Hello, how are you?" his voice had gone soft as if he was talking to a child.

"I'm okay," she said. But he could hear from her voice that she was a little bit shaky.

"And don't worry; I am not calling from home, as I feel that that might not be a good idea." Her voice had changed to a very matter of fact tone. He had always wondered how much Sarah knew, and what she had just said, made him wonder again.

"Do you think it is a good idea me going to the funeral, or the boys for that matter? Whoever bumped her off might not have the best interest in mind for anyone they believe might have been close to Margaret. They might wonder how much we know," Sarah asked.

"How much do you know Sarah?" he wanted to ask but didn't. He didn't want to spoil the surprise, so he said, "Don't worry about that, it has all been taken care of. Please trust me on that one; just meet me on the day at a place we will prearrange."

He could hear her thinking and wondering, but all she said was, "Okay," and sighed.

"Are you really okay Sarah?" he asked again.

"It's just taken me a bit of time getting back into the swing of things that's all. I don't feel like doing anything, to be honest. I guess I will feel better when the funeral is over. And I miss your company." That last sentence just slipped out; she knew she had not intended you say that.

John's heart skipped a beat and he stopped breathing for a moment. And before he could say anything, she said, "Did I say that out loud?"

"I'm glad you did," John said very quietly.

"And I miss you too, so let me know what I can do to rectify that. Maybe a new dress for the lady for the funeral? We could meet somewhere downtown where nobody knows us, get you a dress or an outfit and then have a spot of lunch. How does that sound?" he asked, knowing he was pushing boundaries and being a bit cocky.

"Today?" Sarah asked, "I look awful!"

John could hear the tiredness in her voice, and all he wanted to do was go over to her house and give her a big hug and stroke her hair until she fell asleep.

"Why don't we leave it for tomorrow? Go home, have a rest and I will have some food sent over."

"Okay," Sarah said. She was not going to argue with that, because all she wanted to do was sleep. And if someone else prepared the food she would eat it, although she didn't feel very hungry. How nice to have someone else take care of her for a change.

"Good, I shall have a selection sent over so you don't have to choose now, and then you can pick what you want." He was delighted that she was letting him take care of her a little bit, because that was all he wanted to do, take care of her from now on. And he had expected more resistance, but he had gotten none. That's what he called a result.

"Okay, thank you, bye," she said and hung up. She was so tired, all she could think about, was going back to bed. She had felt like a zombie, ever since she had come back to the city, and she had no idea why. And right now she didn't care; all she wanted to do was sleep.

She had not felt like this since her husband Charlie died. And then when she eventually got over that, she had always been busy and had a purpose to her every day and she had loved it. And now she couldn't care less about anything, and she couldn't care less that she couldn't care less.

As John came off the phone with Sarah, he couldn't help but feel a slight concern. She sounded dead when she spoke, it was the only way he could describe it.

"What was going on with her?" He had one of his guys constantly keeping a watch over her house, as her safety was extremely important to him. And they had all reported that there never were any lights on in her house.

"Was she ill? Was she hiding from someone, or did she lead a double life?" Now that was ridiculous, now his imagination was starting to run wild. Just because he led a double life, didn't mean everybody else did too.

"How could he find out more?" After the funeral, he was going to suggest another trip up to the cabin.

Chapter Eleven

The final touches for both funerals were being organised, and the mob was getting twitchy. No one seemed to know what was going on including himself. Who had killed Margaret? No one knew, apparently. He had had it all so well planned out.

How Margaret would disappear into thin air and the mob would think that someone had bumped her off, and dumped the body somewhere, where it would never be found. He was going to give her a new identity, in another part of the country where no one knew her.

At the time, he had not known about Margaret's sons, she had kept that secret well. How could he have missed that? She must have planned to just present them at the crucial moment of disappearance, where she could insist on them coming too.

Margaret's boys! He had almost forgotten about her boys. They were still with Sarah's sister and husband. That was it! He suddenly had a brilliant idea. He would go and see Sarah to ask her advice about the boys, whether she thought they should come to the funeral or not. It could be a bit tricky as she didn't know about the real funeral, and might think it too risky for them to come.

He would discuss it with Anna, Sarah's sister and then swear her to secrecy. That evening he left his house the way no one would see him, through the back by the garage and down the tunnel, and he came out two blocks away in disguise.

He walked through all the little back streets and alleys to get to Sarah's house, which took him a good half an hour. He went to the back yard of her house, and saw the light on in her kitchen.

"Oh good, she's up, so I don't have to "break" in." He could see her through the window in her dressing gown, by the counter, preparing something. He knocked very gently on the door, not wanting to startle her. She didn't react at all, completely in her own little world. He knocked again, slightly harder this time.

Sarah stopped doing what she was doing for a moment as if she was listening out for something, lifting her head slightly. But then she went back to doing what she had been doing, again. In the end, he opted for a slight knock and calling her name.

"Sarah," he half-whispered with the knock. That did it; she turned around sharpish and opened the door.

"John," she said with a tired disinterested look on her face. And then she just turned around again and carried on with was she was doing, which was preparing a snack. Her behaviour really surprised him, she occurred as if she couldn't care less. He could have been a burglar, a rapist anyone and she had opened the door without checking who it was.

"Are you okay?" he asked.

"What do you want John?" She asked as if he was some kind of nuisance. It really shocked him.

"What is going on with you Sarah?" He asked.

"Oh you mean you don't know?" She was being really sarcastic.

"I thought you knew everything that went on in this neighbourhood." Her voice was sarcastic and accusational, but she still wasn't looking at him, just carried on preparing her snack. John's mind was racing, what was going on? Who was this woman? She seemed to have no resemblance to the Sarah he had got to know, what had she found out or did she already know about him?

He composed himself and said, "Sarah what are you trying to say? You don't seem yourself."

"Oh John, we all know who and what you are. It's just that I fell for your charm for a little while at the cabin, away from all this mess. I just want to go back to my life, before you and that awful night when Margaret was killed."

She turned around very slowly and looked him straight in the eyes and asked, "Did you have her killed? Obviously you wouldn't have done the dirty work yourself! And you were with me in your car when it actually happened, so it would have had to have been one of your men."

She carried on looking at him, challenging him to answer, and her eyes were full of disgust. It was almost unbelievable for him, if anyone else had challenged him like that, he would have shrugged his shoulders and not cared at all what they thought. Or he would have had them dealt with. But Sarah, he couldn't bear for her to think ill of him.

He took a deep breath and said, "I didn't have her killed, I swear on my parent's spirits." It was the only thing he could think of swearing on that he thought she might believe. And as he said it, he could see her being shook out of the trance-like state she had been in.

"Quite the opposite, I had planned to get her away from all of this. Somewhere safe for her, I didn't actually know about her boys at that point. If you will allow me, I will tell you everything about my life," John looked at Sarah pleadingly.

"I just want to sleep, leave me alone. Nothing has been the same since that night," Sarah replied and started to walk towards the stairs heading back to her bedroom. It was then he realised that she had gone into shock and wasn't able to deal with anything.

Probably, as she got back to the city and her house where Margaret had come after her accident, all the emotions of that night must have come flooding back. The police had told him that Margaret had been in a pretty horrific state after the accident, and they thought there was no way she could have dragged herself all the way to Sarah's house.

Someone must have dumped her there; the question was why? Being back in the house must have triggered bad and disturbing memories for Sarah, and being on her own would not have helped.

"Why had he not thought of that before?" She needed looking after. Him, he had seen so many horrific things during his years in the mob that nothing really faced him anymore. And he hadn't seen Margaret's body so he still remembered her how she was before the accident.

John followed Sarah up the stairs, and when he got to her bedroom, she was already lying on her bed staring into space. He sat down next to her and started to stroke her head. At this point, he had nothing to lose and he didn't care how it might be received. She needed looking after.

She had been so amazing with him that night at the cabin when he had gone into meltdown over the memories of his parents. And Sarah accepted his gentle touch without any argument, and then she moved closer and started to cling to him.

He lay down next to her and cradled her, and she kept clinging to him like a frightened child. And his heart was in so much pain over her pain, he could hardly bear it. He had no idea how long they had laid like that, before he heard her breath become steady and he knew she was asleep.

He was so glad one of his guys was watching the house, which meant he didn't have to get up and organise anything. One of many good things about his guys was that they never asked questions about a task, they just did as they were asked. They trusted him and his judgements completely, and he trusted them.

Eventually, he fell asleep too, after holding her, for what seemed an eternity. While he had been lying there listening to her breathing, he had got present to how fragile she was right now. Not the strong self-confident woman he had been infatuated with at first and slowly every day had developed more and more feelings for, he really felt that he loved her already.

It was amazing how one incident could lead to your whole emotional life being turned upside down, which then had a huge impact on the rest of your life. He would really love to know what was going on in her head, so he could help and support her in getting through it, and come out the other side even stronger than before.

After Sarah had got back to the city form the trip with John, and she had walked into her house, everything had felt different. She had come home, made herself a cup of herbal tea and sat down in the parlour. And all of a sudden the memories of that night when Margaret had died had come flooding back.

She had no idea how Margaret had made it the distance from where the accident had taken place, to her house. The state of Margaret had been shocking, the look of which would stay with her for the rest of her life.

Half of Margaret's face was smashed to pieces and the other side was swollen and bruised. One of her arms was broken almost in half, and the bottom part dangling as if it was part of a rag doll. She couldn't walk and was trying to drag herself across Sarah's door step.

Sarah had managed to bring her into the parlour, gently settling her on the floor. She had not wanted to take a chance of trying to get her on to one of the sofas. She was worried that that could do more harm than good with several broken bones, she was sure one of her legs was broken too. And there could have been serious internal damage as well, so she had attempted to make Margaret as comfortable as possible without doing any more harm.

Then she had called an ambulance and held Margaret's hand stroking it gently whilst trying to get as much information out of her as possible. Margaret had seemed delirious and Sarah had not been sure if Margaret knew she was there or where she was.

Margaret had tried to talk but had mainly mumbled, and Sarah had not been able to work out everything that Margaret had been trying to say, but John's name had come up a lot. And it had not all been good.

"You have wanted me gone for a long time now John, so is this your doing? Although this was not what we had planned! I know I deserve it, but couldn't you have done a better job of it so I didn't have to suffer like this? Oh my boys, will you look after my boys please?" She had said and looked at Sarah.

"Of course I will," Sarah had reassured Margaret. Sarah had not known that Margaret had children and had to think fast. She had managed to get the address of where her boys were and their names, and made her promise that she would always look after them if Margaret didn't make it.

And she had immediately thought of her sister Anna and her husband Ray, who she was sure would take care of the boys for now. And the last thing Margaret had said was, "If you need any help with anything, ask John O'Connor, he owes me now."

Sarah had gone with Margaret in the ambulance, and by that time Margaret was unconscious, which Sarah was relieved about. It meant that Margaret could no longer feel any pain. Sarah could tell by the looks on the doctors faces that Margaret's injuries were very serious, and heard them talking about very likely internal bleeding.

They rushed Margaret into a treatment room and asked Sarah to wait in the waiting room. She had not waited very long when one of the doctors came and announced that Margaret had passed away. While she had been at the hospital waiting for news of Margaret's condition, she had called Anna and arranged for the boys to be on the earliest coach possible to Catskill the nearest town to Anna and Ray's farm, and they would pick the boys up from there.

When she had explained to Anna what had happened, Anna had been more than happy to help out with the boys and Sarah had been very relieved to get them out of town that quickly.

She had then rushed to the address that Margaret had given her and had to explain to these two young boys that there mother had been in an accident and had passed away. She didn't want to lie to them; kids always knew when adults lied. And giving them false hope was not an option for her, however hard the truth was.

She had explained that they were going to a farm in the countryside for a little while to a very nice couple that would take good care of them. And that they were not to worry about anything as they would always be taken care of, and that she had known their mother and knew that she had been an amazing woman.

One of the reasons Sarah had got in touch with John regarding Margaret's funeral, was to make him pay for what she believed he had done. When Sarah returned home that morning after having placed the boys safely on the coach to Catskill, she was exhausted mentally, physically and emotionally. And none of it had really sunk in; it was more like a very bad dream or a nightmare.

She had left all her contact details with the hospital staff, so that the police would be able to contact her and interview her as a witness if they needed to. She was hungry and thirsty when she got home, but was too tired to do anything about that and went straight to bed.

Unable to sleep, she had got up and gone for a walk to clear her head, and when she got back she had found John on her door step. The last couple of days after she had come back from the trip with John, she had been reliving that fatal night again and again.

She could not get the picture of the state of Margaret out of her head, "that poor, poor woman had not deserved that. And those poor boys, now having to grow up without a father or a mother." Sarah couldn't bear to be in the living room where she had laid Margaret down, while waiting for the ambulance.

All she wanted to do, was sleep, and forget it ever happened. She also felt ashamed that she had gone away with John and fallen for his charm, knowing that he was probably the one responsible for Margaret's death.

"Obviously he had not got his hands dirty; he had let someone else take care of it while using her as an alibi." She was sure that was why he had offered her a ride home.

"How low could someone steep, to cover up their own dirty work? What had she been thinking, agreeing to come away with him alone! She had been alone with that murderer for days, far away from everyone she knew, he could have killed her! Maybe that had been his intention, but for some reason he had changed his mind? He had really used his charm on her up there at the cabin, with his cooking and attentiveness. What a fool she had been!"

All these thoughts had been going around and around in her head, and it was exhausting. She really felt that she had let herself down, even going near a man like John O'Connor. So to help escape her thoughts and feelings, she slept all the time.

It wasn't as if she could discuss this situation with anyone else, to carry some of the burden. Right now she really wished her husband Charlie had been alive, someone to turn to and talk to. She didn't want to communicate with spirit, because she felt they had let her down.

They should have warned her about going for dinner with Margaret that night, and they should have warned her about John. Or had they warned her and she had missed it, or ignored it? Had she lost her touch? She dreamt that she was running through the woods where she had walked with John, but in the dream she is trying to run away from him, and he is chasing her and calling her name.

"Leave me alone, leave me alone," she was shouting. But instead John grabbed her shoulders and shook her. And in that moment, she woke up, and was staring right into John's face. She screamed so loud that John jumped away as if she had hit him.

"Get out of my house, you murderer," Sarah screamed.

"Sarah, please calm down, you've had a bad dream," John said trying to calm her down. Her scream had almost knocked him to the floor, as he had pulled away and lost his balance at the edge of the side of the bed.

She was angry now, "how dared he tell her to calm down?"

"Get out you deceiving bastard, before I call the police," Sarah said with so much anger and venom that his blood ran cold in his veins.

"Okay, I will leave if that is what you want, but I would rather stay and explain a few things to you," John said as calmly as he could. He was still in shock from her reaction to him just before, and the nasty words she had used. He felt sick to his stomach.

"Why had she turned on him like that? Who had she been talking to? Oh god, he couldn't bear it she if she hated him. He would have to tell her the truth about his life, no matter what it would cost him,"

"Get out," Sarah said again. Now, with so much power and conviction, that he decided to leave it for now.

"Okay I will go, but please when you feel better, let me explain my life to you," and with that he got up and left. As Sarah heard the back door close behind him, she fell down on the bed and started to cry hysterically. Nothing made sense any more.

She wished that Margaret never had been a client of hers, and then none of this would have happened to her. She had been doing just fine, enjoying her little business doing readings, and the freedom that came from being single.

She did miss her husband and parents very much, but she had got used to being on her own. And one thing she had learned was not to dwell on the past, and instead appreciate everything she did have. Her parents had left her the house and half their savings which had been quite substantial, and she also had a small pension as a war widow. And she very much enjoyed the freedom all of that gave her.

Her parents had married late in life, and that's why she lost them so early. She had not missed having a man in her life, at least not until now.

"Damn you John O'Connor, why did you have to show up in my life? How could he be two so very different people?" The person she had been up at the cabin with, and the person he appeared to be here in the city, was two completely different people. And she had got sucked in by this "apparently," lovely caring man with cooking skills persona.

When she had exhausted herself crying, something interesting happened. She felt as if she had let go of the burden of the last few weeks. All the bad, sad and depressing thoughts had evaporated, literally, with her tears and she felt like herself again. She got up, had a bath, got dressed and went out shopping for groceries.

John had quite a big shock when one of his guys reported back to him, that the same day when he had left Sarah in the morning, that afternoon, Sarah had left her house, looking very well and very energetic and gone shopping. He was very glad that Sarah seemed to be feeling better, it was a huge relief. But right now, she didn't want to see him and he had to respect that.

He had to trust that at some point, she would give him the opportunity to explain himself. In the meantime, he would have his guys carry on keeping watch over her. After Sarah had cooked herself dinner and eaten, the most extraordinary thing happened.

It was about 8.30pm and she was sitting in her parlour listening to some music and reading Agatha Christie, (she did like a good murder mystery), when there was a knock at the front door. A very faint one, it was so faint, that she had to stop and listen to work out what it was, and where it was coming from.

It was only when it was repeated that she realised it was a knock on her front door. She went to the door and opened it, and standing outside was a young man, she had never seen before.

"Yes?" She said suspiciously, "Can I help you?"

"I'm really sorry to disturb you ma'am, but may I come in for a moment?" The young man asked. He looked very nervous, terrified even.

"Is everything alright?" Sarah asked wondering what on earth this young man was doing on her doorstep.

"It's about what happened to your friend who died," the young man said almost in tears.

"I think you better come in," Sarah said as her heart sank into her stomach, and she stepped aside to let him in. She took him through to her client room at the back, where they wouldn't be seen from the street.

"Would you like a cup of tea or coffee," Sarah asked.

"No thank you ma'am," he replied. He looked like he wanted the floor to swallow him up, and he was really shaking.

Sarah sat down behind the desk opposite him and asked, "What can I do for you?"

"I don't know where to start, and I have wanted to come and see you ever since it happened. But I was so scared of the consequences of telling you," he answered.

"Telling me what?" Sarah asked, getting really curious about why he was there.

"Your friend," he whispered, "The lady who died." As he said it, her heart dropped into her stomach and she started to feel dizzy.

"Yes, what about her?" She managed to ask.

"Who was this young man, and what was he doing in her house? Oh god, what was he about to tell her?" She wanted to ask a million questions, but was scared of the answers. She could hardly breathe, wondering what was coming next. And to think she had been feeling so much better that very afternoon.

"Please don't hate me. I have been a fool, and I was so afraid that my parents and the police would find out. I don't think I can cope with prison, and my parents would disown me for sure," the young man said. Then the penny dropped.

"Why did you kill her?" Sarah asked.

"I didn't mean to," the young man whispered. The answer startled her.

"What did he mean, he didn't mean to? It was all planned, wasn't it?" Sarah was getting very confused.

"You see, it was my twenty first birthday and my parents had bought me a car, and I had been out partying with my friends. I wanted to impress this one particular girl and I drank too much, and I'm not really that used to drinking.

"I was way too drunk to drive, but didn't want to leave my new car behind, as I didn't want my parents to know that I had drunk too much. So I got in my car, and it wasn't until I started driving that I realised how drunk I was, so I started to speed up to get home quicker.

"I could not see the road clearly, and wasn't even sure how close I was to the sidewalk. I completely miscalculated the curb going around a bend at high speed, drove right up on to the sidewalk and hit your friend. She had no chance, as she could not have seen me coming.

"The thump of the impact I felt when I hit her, will stay with me for the rest of my life." The silence in the room when he had finished talking was deafening. Sarah was in a state of shock, and found it very hard to take it all in. Her mind was racing.

"Had Margaret's death, actually been a random accident, and not a well-planned assassination? Was the whole neighbourhood mob going crazy over nothing? Well, not nothing, a life had been lost, but the worry of who did it, was for nothing."

Sarah started to laugh hysterically, and she could not stop. She was rocking up and down like a crazy person. The young man looked at her absolutely bewildered.

"Had the woman gone stir crazy?" He had no idea what to do, so he just sat there staring at the floor, wondering what would happen once she stopped laughing. Sarah tried to stop several times, but couldn't.

Every time she slowed down and caught her breath, she got the giggles again. Finally, after about five minutes, she was done.

She looked at the young man with an innocent smile and said, "Sorry about that, I couldn't help it." As she was saying that and looking at the boy, she realised that he was terrified. And it must have taken an enormous amount of courage to come there and tell her what he had done.

"Why did you come here to tell me this, when you knew that the likelihood of anyone finding out the truth was almost zero? And how did you know I was her friend, and where I live?" More and more questions were coming to her mind.

"She kept saying your name over and over again, so I asked her where you were, and she gave me your address," the young man answered.

"She remembered my address?" Sarah was stunned.

"After the hit Margaret had taken and the state she was in, she still had remembered her address. Extraordinary!"

Then the penny dropped again, "So you dropped her off here?" Sarah asked.

"Yes," he said very quietly, glad that Sarah had calmed down.

"It all makes sense now," she said talking to herself.

"I couldn't, for the life of me, figure out, how she had managed to get here that night. Now that bit makes sense."

"I'm sorry, he whispered," crying quietly into his hands, "I didn't mean to hurt anyone, I am so sorry." She almost felt sorry for him, but she had no time for the recklessness of youth. Because of his fear of his parents, he had caused an unnecessary death, and left two young boys without their mother after already losing their father.

She had gone very quiet, so he looked up trying to "read" what was going on over there with her. She was sitting in deep thought, staring into space. He could handle almost anything but the silent treatment. He would have preferred it if she had been screaming and shouting, or even hitting him.

"What are you going to do?" He eventually asked. His words startled her, and brought her back into the room.

"I don't know," she answered and let out a big sigh.

"I really don't know, what are you expecting me to do?" She asked, throwing the ball back in his court.

"I don't know, I just want it to be over," he said.

"Over? What do you mean over? It will never be over for those two boys, who have lost their mother!" She was angry now.

"This boy had come here to ease his own pain, no one else's! I can't live with what I did and had to own up, and I will take whatever punishment comes my way," he said.

"And then you hope it will be over for you?" She was seething with anger now. She didn't even know she had this much anger in her. It was as if all her sadness, upset and stress of the last few weeks was all surfacing at once and turning into anger. And all of it was now directed towards this young man, who was the cause of it all. It hit him, what she had just said.

"Yes he had come there hoping to feel better, hoping someone would forgive him, as he was unable to forgive himself."

"What's your name, and where do you live?" Sarah asked the young man.

93

"My name is James Hillman, and I live with my parents on Upper East Side."

"Well James, I will have to think about what I want to do with all this new information. And then I will be in touch, to let you know," Sarah concluded.

"But how will you know that I won't just disappear?" He knew he shouldn't have asked that question but he couldn't help himself.

"Well here's the thing James. Wherever you go, what you caused will haunt you. So you can run but you can't hide, and it will be harder and harder for you to come back and face the music. And you will be away from all your family and friends, the choice is yours. Right now I don't particularly care either way," Sarah stated.

She got up out of her chair and said, "I would like you to leave now."

"Yes of course," James was out of his chair in no time, happy to get away from this unpredictable woman.

"I just want you to know, I will not disappear. So whenever you are ready, let me know what you are going to do, and I will cooperate fully," and with that Sarah followed James out into the hall way.

At the front door, James turned around and said, "Thank you for your time and again I am really, really sorry for your loss."

"Good bye Mr Hillman," Sarah said coldly and shut the door behind him. For a moment Sarah felt completely blank, and walked like a zombie into the parlour. She sat down in her favourite chair, breathing deep into her stomach for a little while.

"Well, the mystery of what had happened to Margaret, had definitely been solved by Mr James Hillman of Upper East Side, coming forward. And she now had an answer to how Margaret had managed to get herself to her front door, after her fatal accident. Had no one seen the accident? Or Mr Hillman getting Margaret into his car, or him getting her out of the car and on to Sarah's front steps?"

Another question that came to her mind was, "How much extra damage had Mr Hillman possibly caused Margaret by moving her in and out of his car? Could she have survived if an ambulance had been called straight away? No point in speculating about that now, because it was too late. That stupid, stupid reckless boy, she felt so angry with him."

Then it struck her, "What about John and the rest of the mob?" No wonder they were all going nuts wondering who had done it, none of them were responsible. How ironic! The whole of the mob watching over their shoulder for nothing! Served them right, the nasty fuckers! Maybe she wouldn't tell a soul, maybe it would stay her and James Hillman's little secret!

Let them all suffer, like they made so many people suffer on a daily basis. Including John, because he had been planning to get rid of her, had he not? She had been extremely rude to him earlier, mainly because she thought he had had Margaret killed. But if he had planned to, but James Hillman accidentally had got there first, he was still a nasty piece of work.

Whatever would she find out next? What about the funeral, should she go or not? John might not want her there after this morning's little performance. Quite frankly, she didn't care. She would say good bye to Margaret in her own way.

Chapter Twelve

John's guy reported back to John that a young man had turned up at Sarah's front door that evening. That Sarah had let him in, and he had stayed for about an hour, and they had not been in the parlour as the lights had not been on in there. John's guy did not know who the young man was.

John, of course, was curious about who this young man was, but he was much more concerned about Sarah's expressed opinion of him. The young man could simply be a client.

"Why had Sarah turned on him like that? What did she know, or think she knew? The funeral was in a couple of days. Should he delay it which was easily done, or trust that she would have calmed down by then?"

Luckily, they had spoken a lot about the funeral arrangements on the way back from the cabin, so he knew roughly what Sarah had in mind. As he hadn't been able to get much sense out of her since they got back.

The main funeral was no big deal, it was the other one, the real one that he had planned for Sarah and the boys, which needed to be arranged properly. But Sarah didn't know about that one, so he couldn't tell her.

"Hey Sarah, I need to know whether you are coming or not, so I can let them know there out in the sticks, where I have arranged the surprise one for you."

He really wished he knew what was going through her mind, so he would know how to approach her again. He wasn't a man who gave up easily, as a rule; he never gave up on anything. But with Sarah it was different, because he was emotionally attached to her.

Now that he had found her, he simply could not imagine his life without her. But the way things were going, he would have to. His guys were filling him in on what had been going on in the neighbourhood while he had been gone, and still nobody had a clue about who had bumped off Margaret. Even the police had nothing to go on. No one had seen or heard anything that night; it was as if the whole neighbourhood had been blind and deaf.

Strangely enough, it had been Margaret's job to be the eyes and ears of that neighbourhood. John's guys were exploring many different theories, but he had stopped listening and had drifted off, thinking about Sarah again.

For him, the most likely explanation was that the police had got rid of her, thinking she had become too much of a liability. And they could more easily cover their tracks by not investigating, by outwardly pretending to do so.

Sarah's thought were focused on James Hillman and his confession.

"What should she do with the information the young man James Hillman had given her? Or more to the point, what should she do with him? Hand him over to the police? But if she did that, they might find out about Margaret's boys as she had let that slip to James Hillman in her anger. Get John to deal with him? That would put John to the test, by telling him and let John decide James Hillman's fate.

"Now that was actually not a bad idea, because she herself would be spared having to make the decision. And it would give her a clue about how John really felt about Margaret's death."

By the time she went to bed, she still hadn't decided on what she was going to do.

Sarah woke up very early the next morning, and the first thought she had was, "What if John had sent the young man and it was all lies, in order for him to look innocent in her eyes? But then again, why would he really care what she thought of him?"

Then she remembered what he had said the previous day before he left; "Okay I will go, but please when you feel better, let me explain my life to you."

"What a strange thing to say, what was there about his life to explain?" His life seemed pretty obvious to her, and probably the rest of the neighbourhood too. He was a rich bully that together with the rest of the mob terrorised and terrified the neighbourhood with his protection money demands, violence and killings. And he was a coward, because he never did his own dirty work or so she believed anyway.

So whatever his reasons were for choosing this kind of life, would not justify to her him doing and living it. So why did he need her approval, she was nobody in society? John decided to do what he would normally do in any circumstance, and that was to not take no for an answer. To go and see Sarah, and just tell her where to meet him for the funeral, and still keep the real funeral as a surprise.

He had already organised with Sarah's sister to bring Margaret's boys to the real funeral. But had not told her that he was having problems with Sarah, as he didn't want to worry her.

The day before the funeral, he sent one of his guys around to Sarah's house with a delivery from Romanos restaurant. When Sarah opened the door the "delivery man" told her that his boss John O'Connor would be at her back door shortly to see her.

"Shall I bring the box to the kitchen for you, ma'am?" he then asked politely.

"No you cannot," Sarah answered sharply, took the box from the man and kicked the door shut in his face, while holding the box still.

The "delivery man" blew out a whistle to himself and said, "That is one pissed dame."

And then he laughed, "Good luck with that boss," as he wondered what the boss had done to enrage this dame.

"Probably the usual stuff, using her then dumping her," he guessed.

By the time Sarah reached her kitchen, John was already outside the back door. He had decided not to let himself in, as he didn't want to set her off on another rage. Him coming round uninvited and unannounced was probably enough to make her angry with him again, which was something he could do without.

For a moment, he didn't think she was going to let him in, as Sarah only glanced in his direction. Then put the box down on the counter and started to empty the content. Then she slowly turned around, walked over to the door and opened it without even looking at him.

Turned around on her heel and walked back to the counter and said, "You might as well set the table as you have brought lunch for two, and then you can explain to me why you have come when I expressly asked you to stay away."

John was smiling to himself as he loved the fact that she was "back". Whatever had been going on for her the other day was gone, and right now he didn't care how. Today because he had put on the mask of John O'Connor the big boss, he felt his usual cocky self, and felt he could handle anything she threw at him.

"Well you didn't say for how long I should stay away, and with the funeral being tomorrow, I thought it was time to reconnect," John said very matter-of-factly.

"The arrogant sun of a bitch," was the thought going through Sarah's head.

But she said, "And what makes you so sure I am going to the funeral Mr O'Connor?" John flinched for a moment, when he heard her use his surname rather than his first name. She really wanted to keep it formal.

"Okay, he could play that game too." For him, it was most important that she came to the funeral. The "real" one. He had arranged that especially for her and Margaret's boys, and he wanted to see her reaction to him having gone through all that trouble.

"What have you got there?" She asked pointing at the parcel in his hand.

"More food? I think there is enough in the other box, and are you going to lay the table or not?" He had to hide a grin, at her arrogant game playing; he could see that she was finding it hard to keep it up, and that she was curious to find out why he really was there. That gave him the edge, which filled him with confidence.

And Sarah was thinking, "I know something you don't know and that gives me power over you Mr O'Connor, because you think you know everything about everyone in this neighbourhood."

She still hadn't decided what to do with the information that had come to light the day before, when James Hillman had paid her a visit. So they both sat down at the lunch table feeling fairly cocky and confident, as if they each had the upper hand.

"I will show you what's in the other parcel after lunch Mrs Steel," he replied to her question. If she had reacted to him keeping it formal, she didn't show it. They ate in silence for a while, and then John broke the ice.

"I have arranged a taxicab to pick you up at the corner of your street, to take you to the church."

"I can make my own way thank you, if I decide to go," Sarah stated.

"I know you have been concerned with being seen at the funeral, but you don't have to worry, I have taken care of that. And you do want to pay your respect, don't you?" John asked ignoring her statement.

"I can pay my respects in my own way, without being there. The church will possibly be full of your kind, and I don't agree with yours or any of their lifestyles," Sarah replied. Those last words were like being hit with a steel bar in the solar plexus.

"Jesus, did she hate him that much?" He thought. He was so tempted to tell her about his life, and why he did what he did. But this was not the right time.

He would have to carefully plan that moment in case she didn't take it in the right way.

"What about Margaret's boys, are they coming?" Sarah asked very unexpectedly.

"Eh, no we are doing something separate for them," he hesitated as he had not been prepared for that question. He should have been, as it was a perfectly natural question for her to ask.

"Can't I come to that instead?" Sarah asked.

"I tell you what, if you come to the big one, I will take you to the one with the boys as well." John answered, very proud of himself, for thinking so fast on his feet. Sarah looked at him for a long moment, trying to work him out.

"Why is it so important to you that I go?" She asked.

"Because it is," he answered with conviction, but no explanation.

"And if you tell me you have nothing to wear, I have already solved that for you," he added gesturing in the direction of the parcel he had brought with him, that he had left on the coffee table.

"You must mistake me for one of the many other women in your life," Sarah said in an icy voice.

John went bright red like a school boy and said, "Jesus Sarah, was that really necessary?"

The words were out of his mouth before he could think, and then he added, "I can assure you, that you do not compare to any other woman I have ever known!"

He wanted to add, "That is why I am totally and utterly in love with you, because you are one in a million." But he didn't as he didn't want to look more of a fool than he already did.

"I already know that, and I am glad you do too," Sarah replied calmly.

She could not work John out, "Was he or was he not interested in her? It didn't really matter though, as she was not interested in anything he had to offer.

"Could I be in any kind of danger going to the funeral tomorrow?" She then asked.

"No, I can assure you, you won't be." He could say that with real conviction, because he knew she wasn't going to be at the one she thought she was going to be at.

"Okay, I will come as I want to try and suss out who killed her so cowardly," she said wanting to see his reaction. But there wasn't one.

"So that is settled then," John said matter-of-factly. He could be very hard to read, she guessed it was years of practice of being a "poker" face in his line of work, if you could call it that.

"How was one person, so capable of being two so very different characters? On one hand he was a cold blooded murderer and one of the heads of the mob in his neighbourhood. On the other hand he was kind, gentle and generous host who cooked, cleaned and even cried."

"What are you thinking Sarah?" John asked, pulling her away from her thoughts. His question startled her; she had been completely absorbed in her own thoughts.

"I could answer that, but I don't think you would particularly like the answer," she replied being as matter of fact as him.

"Is it going to kill me?" He asked with that cheeky grin on his face, she had come to know so well. He had not been prepared for the reaction he got, which to him, was just a silly flippant remark. Sarah looked at him in sheer horror.

"I don't think that is very funny, considering the circumstances why you are here," she whispered suddenly looking very pale. John realised that it had been very unfortunate and stupid choice of words.

"I am sorry," he whispered back, "That was very insensitive and stupid of me." He looked like a little boy who had been severely told off by his parents.

Sarah recalled the time when he had come down to the jetty to clear the air after their incident in the stream, on their last walk up at his cabin. And she remembered how she had felt about him, after those few days up there.

It was a rollercoaster ride knowing this man, and she didn't know how much more she could take.

"In answer to your question," she started, "I was wondering how you could be two such different people. A cold blooded murderer, and a kind, gentle and generous host."

The words hit him hard, "A cold blooded murderer is that how you see me?" He could hardly get the words out. This man brought out the worst in her on so many levels that she had never known before. And his expression surprised her; he really did have a vulnerable side.

"Well I assume that is part of your job description, is it not?" She asked. She no longer felt as confident as earlier.

"Don't get fooled," she said to herself, "This man is an expert in playing games and deceiving people. Getting you to believe his act and taking the conversation in his preferred direction."

"Like I said yesterday, when the time is right, I will explain my life to you. I owe you that much," John replied.

"You don't owe me anything Mr O'Connor. Once tomorrow is over. We can go our separate ways, and get on with our lives," was Sarah's reply. The thought of never seeing her again, felt like a fist in the gut and a knife in his heart at the same time.

But he kept his composure, "Hopefully tomorrow would win her over a little bit."

"Let's not argue today Sarah, let's just prepare for tomorrow. And focus on a good send off for Margaret," John pleaded.

"Okay, let's call it truce until the day after tomorrow," Sarah replied with a tired sigh, and without looking at him, started to clear the table.

"Would you like me to do the dishes for you, so you can open your parcel?" He asked. He really wanted to see her face, when she opened it.

"No thanks, I would like you to leave now," she said suddenly feeling a real need to be on her own. It was exhausting playing this game with him.

"Okay I will leave you alone, good afternoon Sarah." And with that he left by the back door, the same way he had come in. He would just have to imagine her face, when she opened the parcel. Mind you in the mood she was in, she might get really angry with him again.

Daring to go shopping for her, he could almost hear her; "How dare you think you know what I want? And how do you know my size?" Blah, blah, blah, anger, anger, anger. He had to smile to himself. He thought he knew her so well, but in reality he didn't know her at all. He was tired of this life, always pretending to be someone else, it was time to quit.

After Sarah had done the dishes, she sat down in her favourite chair by the window in her parlour, as she often did. Thinking about the funeral the next day, she again questioned if it was a good idea, her going.

"Wouldn't everybody who would be there wonder what she was doing there? And start to wonder about her connection to Margaret, and what she may know? Could it put her in danger, was ultimately what she was asking herself. Did John want her there to take the spotlight off him?"

As she was having these thoughts, her eyes started to wander around the room, and landed on the parcel John had brought with him. She got up and walked over to the parcel on the coffee table and opened it. It was wrapped in brown paper, and underneath, there was a beautiful box which had the name of one of the expensive boutiques in town.

She was very surprised; she really wasn't expecting that. She opened the lid, and inside, beautifully laid out, was a simple but elegant black dress, a pair of black shoes, black silk stockings, a black hat and a black silk scarf. There was a card in one corner in an envelope, she picked it up and opened the envelope. It read:

Dear Sarah,

In case you didn't feel like going shopping, and wasn't sure you had something to wear to the funeral.

P.S. Please forgive me for being so forward.

John xxx

If he had been a normal man with a normal job, she would have been thrilled at the thought and consideration. But considering the circumstances, she was just left with a question; "What's in it for you Mr O'Connor?"

But two could play this game; she would wear the outfit unless it didn't fit. And she still knew something he didn't know, and that still gave her the upper hand.

The dress was beautiful, very simple, very good quality, just the kind of thing she would have chosen herself, but obviously, not at that price. She could only guess how much this particular dress would cost based on where it was bought.

The shoes were exquisite made from the best Italian leather and the scarf was pure silk. She tried it all on, and it all fitted perfectly.

"How did he manage that?" She wondered. He had probably had one of his guys come and "borrow" some of her clothes, while they had been away, to check out her measurements and her shoe size.

She was convinced that that was what he had done, or hopefully it had been Rose going through her wardrobe. She did have a funeral outfit she could use, but it would be a shame to waste such a beautiful outfit, she thought and smiled.

She was also surprised at herself and who she had become, she didn't like the way she wanted to get one over on John. It had become a tit for tat game now, she wanted to knock him down a peg or two.

"Did he really think he could get away with murder? Although technically he didn't kill Margaret, it had been his plan to do so, had it not? Why did the first man she had felt any interest in at all, in years, had to be someone like him?"

After the funeral she had to get away, she would sell up and move away. The city did not excite her in the same way anymore. For the money she would get for her house, she could buy a cottage or a small house somewhere in the country near her sister Anna, and live a very comfortable life.

"Let's just get tomorrow out of the way," she said to herself, "and then I can start to make some plans for the future." If Margaret hadn't been killed, she probably would have carried on in the same way she had been for years to come.

The whole situation had made her take stock of her life in a way she wouldn't have done otherwise. It could be an exciting new start for her, close to her beloved sister. After hanging up the dress, scarf and hat, ready for the next day, she left the house and went to a telephone booth.

She dialled John's number and Rose answered, "O'Connor's residence."

"May I speak to Mr O'Connor please," Sarah said very calmly.

"Who may I say is calling?" Rose asked knowing full well it was Sarah Steel. "Mrs Steel," Sarah replied.

"Just one moment please and I will see if he is free," Rose said. Rose had no idea if John was in or not, he had been in and out so many times that day, she had lost track. He had not eaten any of the food she had prepared, which always worried Rose.

Rose found John in his bedroom, looking through his wardrobe.

"John?" Rose called his name gently and knocked on the door even though it was open. John's bedroom was large and masculine in décor and colours, a mahogany bed and matching wardrobe, with a beautiful Persian carpet on the floor in deep colours picking up the colours of the furniture.

His bed was unusually wide which he had had custom made for a very specific reason. He had never found a woman of any interest beyond the physical until now, so he preferred a large bed where he could spread himself out, without having to cuddle up to the occasional woman who would share his bed.

He had also believed that the task he had set himself would be a lifelong one, and because of its nature and his parent's fate, he had not wanted to bring children into the world.

There were plenty of women who loved his lifestyle, who would offer their "services" for as long as he wanted, in return for some nice dinners, clothes, shoes, handbags and jewellery. But unfortunately, the kind of woman he had been after was not really available to him and the lifestyle and career he had chosen.

It was by pure chance that he had met Sarah, but it was obvious from her behaviour yesterday and today, that she had no interest in him. She despised his lifestyle and career, she thought he was a despicable human being who killed and bullied people. And she was right, but she didn't know why he did it.

He was dying to tell her, to come clean about everything. But there could be huge consequences, which he had to prepare for. First of all, she might not care about the reasons why he had chosen to do what he had done; secondly, could he trust her?

He had thought he could, but the way she had completely turned on him, he was no longer so sure. And she seemed quite unstable at the moment, which didn't help his situation at all.

If he came clean and told her everything, he would have to prepare for the worst, and have everything ready to deal with it if the shit hit the fan.

"Yes Rose, what is it?" He asked, carrying on doing what he was doing.

"Mrs Steel is on the phone," Rose told him.

"Sarah?" He asked turning around wide eyed and excited, but in the next moment trying to compose himself.

"I shall answer it here, thank you Rose," trying to be nonchalant, but he couldn't fool Rose and they knew it.

But Rose left him with his dignity intact and said, "Very well, I shall hang up downstairs," acting all matter-of-factly like she would if anyone else called.

"Hello Sarah, what can I do for you?" He asked keeping his voice very business-like. If she wanted distance, he would give her distance for now anyway.

"We didn't agree on a meeting place for tomorrow," Sarah said matching his tone of voice.

"We did, I told you where I would have you picked up," John said sounding slightly irritated.

"Did you? I can't remember or isn't it better if I go own my own? I'm not sure being associated with you, is a good thing for me," her voice was full of judgement.

His first thought was; "Shall I tell her about the real funeral, that I am really taking her too? Was that the only way to get her there?"

Before he could make up his mind, Sarah sighed and said, "I give in, I will get in the taxicab and meet you at the pickup point tomorrow."

"Oh good, I 'm glad," John replied.

"But you can't drop me off right outside," Sarah said.

"Don't worry, I will not drop you off anywhere near the church," as he said it he thought, "Shit that was not very clever, as she would probably think, why bother if she had to walk far anyway."

"I will see you tomorrow," was all Sarah replied and hung up. "And hopefully that will be last time I see you Mr O'Connor," she thought to herself. John didn't care that Sarah had hung up on him, she was coming the next day and hopefully he would score some brownie points. Hopefully enough for her to give him some time to explain his life to her.

John went to bed with a hopeful heart that night, while Sarah did the opposite. She was dreading the funeral and having to be in the same room as possibly the entire mob of the neighbourhood. Or maybe they would all stay away, not wanting to be associated with Margaret in any way.

Chapter Thirteen

Sarah was up early the next morning taking her time getting ready and preparing herself to say her good byes to a woman she hardly knew, and whose life was pretty much a mystery to her. She did a long meditation to keep herself calm, and asked that the spirits would guide Margaret on her journey back home to the spirit world.

When she was ready, she left the house and walked to the corner of her street where the taxicab was waiting, to take her to the meeting point with John. She was right on time at 10 am and John was waiting in the car, watching her, as she came walking towards him.

He thought she looked stunning in the outfit he had bought her, "What an elegant and gracious woman she is, and with some fire in her." He had to smile to himself, remembering her angry outburst, directed at him a couple of days ago.

He had taken his private car, which no one associated with him, because he wanted to do the driving himself. He also wore a kind of hat that he would never wear and sun glasses, so there was very little chance of him being recognised by anyone.

"Good morning John," Sarah said as she arrived at the car.

"Do you want me in the front or the back?" she asked. "The front seat will look less suspicious I think," John answered.

"Most of the mob know the rich ladies in town, and if you sit in the back, I will look like your chauffer, and that will draw more attention from a lot of people. With you in the front, we will look like a couple," John said matter-of-factly. And silently he said to himself, "I wish."

"Yes you are right, I will sit in the front," Sarah said and got into the car. As soon as Sarah got in the car and was settled, John took off, heading in the totally opposite direction from the church.

"Where are you going?" Sarah asked, slightly alarmed by his action.

"I am afraid I got you here under false pretences Sarah. But don't be alarmed, there is nothing untoward going on. I have a surprise for you," John replied. Sarah could feel the panic welling up in her.

"Oh my god, he is going to kill me, and no one will ever know what happened to me." As far as she was concerned, John was capable of anything, and had probably done this sort of thing before.

"How could she be so stupid, of course she was a liability, she knew too much, and she was no longer willing to play ball."

"John, where are we going?" Her voice was barely a whisper. John turned to her with a smile on his face, and then he saw the fear in her eyes, and her body was shaking.

"Sarah, please don't be alarmed," he was mortified that she was that fearful of him.

"I am taking you to the real funeral for Margaret in the country, and her boys are coming too." He had to tell her in the state she was in, nothing else would work he decided.

"But, would she believe him? How could she be so afraid of him?"

"The real funeral? What do you mean the real funeral?" She felt confused.

"I have arranged a funeral for Margaret in the country, so that you and her boys can attend and be safe. And I thought that is probably what Margaret would have wanted too. The one here in town, has no body in the coffin," he tried to explain.

The words came out fast and all wrong, he was racing to get it all out as quickly as possible to calm her down. But he was not making a good job of it. Sarah had calmed down a bit while John was attempting to explain himself, and started to become cynical about it all.

"You must have friends in high places, if you can organise a funeral without a body," her voice now as cold as ice.

"I am beginning to realise what you really think of me, it is finally sinking in. And yes, I have contacts from all walks of life; it is part of my job. And I really wanted to give Margaret a good send off, and for her boys to be able to say good bye peacefully and quietly. And I wanted to include you Sarah, as you were a very good friend to her in the end. So just this one time, can you trust me please, and I will promise you we will have as lovely a day as is possible under the circumstances," John asked nicely.

There was something in John's voice that made Sarah stop her own thoughts, and take note of what he was saying. "Was it guilt that had made him organise this? Was it true, or was he really just trying to convince her to come with him, so he could bump her off?"

In that moment, when she asked herself that question, she automatically did something she had not done for a few days. She linked with spirit, and her number one guide came through, to let her know she was safe.

"The rest you have to work out for yourself," her guide told her. Eddie was her number one spirit guide, who had been with her since birth, and would stay with her until her departure and possibly beyond.

"Okay John, let's make this day count for Margaret's soul and her boys," and in that moment when she said that, she knew she was in the right place for this particular day.

"Great! Thank you for your generosity," John said with a huge sigh. It was a big load off his shoulders, that Sarah had changed her mind. It was possibly the very last day he would ever spend with Sarah and he didn't want to fight or argue with her. Instead, he wanted to give her a day to remember.

They both finally relaxed into their seats, and they both had a little smile on their faces, each one for different reasons.

John, because he now felt that his day seem to finally go the way he had planned it to go, and he might get the opportunity to tell her the truth about his life.

Sarah, because she now felt very happy about Margaret getting a quiet and peaceful send off, far away from the troubled life she had led.

It took an hour or so to get to the small village of Sleepy Hollow, Westchester County, same county as John's cabin. That is why he had chosen it, as he knew of it and had always loved the beautiful Old Dutch stone church there.

The whole village was very beautiful and picturesque, a perfect setting for a peaceful funeral. It was an absolutely enchanted and lovely little village, and Sarah was so very happy that she had decided to trust the situation, and come along.

"John, it is absolutely beautiful here, I know Margaret would have loved it. She is probably looking down on us right now, smiling," Sarah said.

John wanted to say, "I knew you would like it, you stubborn so and so," but instead he said, "I am glad you approve."

Sarah's sister Anna had been aware of the plans for this funeral, but had kept it to herself on John's request. She had very much enjoyed having Margaret's boys, even though they were mourning the loss of their mother.

In reality, they had not seen a lot of her when she was alive, as she had been working all hours. She had constantly been rushing off any time of the day or night, so they had been left with charitable neighbours most of the time.

Henry the oldest one was a very serious young man aged ten. His younger brother Thomas, who was seven, was a little chatter box. Neither of them seemed to understand that their mother was gone forever; the finality of death is almost incomprehensible at such a young age. And now having been on a farm in the countryside with Sarah's sister Anna and her husband Ray, had been a real adventure for the boys, and had taken their mind off their mother a little bit.

As soon as Sarah had left the hospital after Margaret had passed, she had gone to find Henry and Thomas. On the way she had called her sister, to see if it was possible for her and Ray to take care of the two boys for a little while.

Anna and Ray had wanted children for years without any joy, and Sarah could not think of two better people to take care of Margaret's boys, in that moment. And the time Henry and Thomas had spent on the farm so far, was one of the most stable times they had had in their young lives.

Anna and Ray had tried to explain to the boys, that their mother had passed away, but they were not entirely sure the boys had understood. Henry and Thomas were so used to being taken care of by many different people and couples in their neighbourhood that a few days or weeks away from their mother didn't occur as very strange to them.

John drove up to the church and parked the car on the road alongside the stonewall surrounding the graveyard. As Sarah and John got out of the car and walked on to the path leading up to the church door, Anna, Ray, Henry and Thomas came towards them.

They had arrived about ten minutes earlier, and had already been inside the church to look at the flower arrangements.

Thomas, in all his innocence, had turned to Ray and asked him, "Is my mother in heaven now?"

"She sure is, with one guardian angel either side of her," Ray had answered as he ruffled Thomas's hair. As Ray said that, Anna observed Henry's face twist in pain, as if for the first time it had dawned on him, that his mother was gone.

Henry had absolutely loved and adored his mother, and had always missed her whenever she left the house or any house or apartment she left him and Thomas in. Henry was a very intuitive young boy, who knew that his mother worked hard to feed and clothe himself, Thomas and her, and keep a roof over their heads.

He often also felt that the work she was doing wasn't entirely safe. He felt very protective towards his mother, and had often offered to walk her to wherever she was going, if it was after dark. And Margaret had used to look at him, with total love and devotion, and gently tell him that she would be fine, and to look out for his younger brother instead.

It used to pain him to know that what she was really saying was, you are too young, but thank you so much for caring. He had wished that he had been older, so that he could have gone out to work and looked after her instead.

He had truly loved his mother; she had always been there for him. Maybe not always in body but always in spirit, everything she did she had done for them he knew that. She had never spoken about their father, and he could not remember him.

Henry had been in denial about his mother's death, until that moment in the church, when his younger brother Thomas had asked Ray if she now was in heaven. And in that moment it had dawned on him, that he would never see her again. And he would never hear her soft voice again, trying to soothe him or feel her gentle ruffle of his hair, when he wanted to protect her.

He didn't know what to do in that moment, because he didn't want his younger brother to see his pain and despair. He now had to be strong for his brother, and his mother was no longer there to comfort him. He felt so lost and alone, everybody around him right now, was strangers to him.

His mum had been the most beautiful woman he knew, and the kindest one.

"What was he going to do without her?"

In the last year or so, whenever she had been at home, she would sit down with him, telling him stories about the neighbourhood, and teaching him what to look out for to be safe and survive.

He had loved those moments when he had her full attention, feeling her love and being allowed to be a child. Most of the time, he was being a parent to his younger brother. He had never blamed his mother for leaving them alone or with others so much of the time; he knew she was earning a living to support them.

He could still smell her, which was a great comfort to him. She had always smelled so good, and always dressed so beautifully in his eyes. Margaret had told her boys that she was a housekeeper for a rich lady, and when she had to go out in the evenings, she had told them that the rich lady was having a dinner party and she had to help out.

That way, the boys never asked her where she was going, and they were protected, if anyone should ever happen to ask them any questions.

"Can we come to the dinner party too mummy?" Thomas had asked once.

Margaret had smiled and said, "They don't have children at dinner parties in that house unfortunately, but I will take you out for dinner one night I promise." And Henry remembered their mum taking them out for dinner several times to make up for her absence. Those had been happy times.

"Henry, are you alright?" Anna's voice brought him back to the present moment.

"I miss her," he said with tears in his eyes. He had not planned to let anyone know how he felt, as he wanted to be strong for his brother, but when he had observed Thomas and how he had behaved after their mother's death, he didn't seem to be affected at all.

Thomas saw all of life as an adventure and he was used to meeting and being cared for by new people all the time. He had probably seen their mother as a stranger who came and went like everyone else. Or it hadn't sunk in yet that she was never coming back, just as it hadn't for Henry up until now seeing the coffin in the church.

Thomas had also loved staying with Anna and Ray, and saw Ray as a bit of a hero the way he handled everything on the farm. Ray had taken Thomas with him everywhere he went, and had let him "help out," and Thomas would hang on Ray's every word.

Henry on the other hand, had stayed around the house helping Anna out. He had a lot of respect for women, seeing them as strong loving creatures.

Unlike the men in his neighbourhood, who he thought were all gangsters and bullies. Henry became aware that Anna was still in front of him looking worried, waiting for an answer. She had been so good to him, as he had been hanging around the house with her. He had not once felt in the way, or that she was annoyed that he was there.

Considering they had been dumped on them without any warning, and they were both busy keeping the farm going. Anna had talked to him in the same gentle voice that his mum had, for him women were amazing, with such a huge capacity for giving love. But she was not his mother, so he felt uncomfortable being vulnerable in her presence.

He wanted to show Anna that he was a man, and could handle anything life threw at him. Unfortunately he knew Anna could see right through his façade, and he knew that if he broke down now, the floodgates would open and he would not be able to stop crying.

And who was going to pick up the pieces when they got back to the city, and he would have to support his little brother any way he could? They could end up in a work house or children's home, and that in Henry's eyes was worse than death.

He would rather work day and night running errands, working on building sites carrying bricks, anything to keep a roof over their heads and be independent. He knew he could do it if he had to, his mother had told him how to survive in the city.

"I'm alright Anna, I really am, thanks for asking," Henry finally replied. Anna smiled at him and put her arm around his shoulders. She knew he was suffering in silence, to hold it together for his brother. And she didn't want to push him to the point of breakdown, not yet anyway.

Once it had been decided who was going to take care of those wonderful two boys permanently, and Henry felt safe, that would be the right time for Henry to grieve properly.

"Come on, let's go outside in the sunshine and wait for your mum's friends, one of which you have already met, my sister Sarah," Anna said to Henry as she led him out of the church. John and Sarah were walking up the path to the church, and Anna, Ray, Henry and Thomas came towards them.

Sarah was searching her sister's face for an indication of how the mood was in her camp. Sarah had spoken to Anna intermittently since the boys had been with her and Ray, from various public telephones, so she couldn't be listened in on.

Sarah knew the boys were very well looked after, as Anna and Ray had always wanted children, but had never been blessed with any. They lived on a small self-sufficient farm, so the boys would want for nothing of their basic needs.

Anna looked back at Sarah and gave her a nod, that everything was as good as it could be at that moment in time. Sarah really admired her sister; she was

113

such a calm and gentle woman. Seeing the way Henry was looking at Anna, she knew she had made the right decision, to send the boys to her.

"Hello Henry, hello Thomas, it is really good to see you again. Let me introduce you to one of your mother's friends, Mr John O'Connor," Sarah said and gestured towards John.

"Very nice to finally meet you both, although I would have wished it had been under different circumstances," John said and shook their hands in turn while saying, "Henry, Thomas."

Henry looked John straight in the eyes and then gave him the once over, while his eyes were saying, "I know your type; the neighbourhoods back in the city are full of guys like you, and you don't impress me."

John had to admire the boy, he had guts, and he was not going to take any nonsense from anyone. And he thought this very young man with such a strong character, would always land on his feet. And John would make sure of that, he would do whatever he could for both the brothers. He owed Margaret that, and he also really wanted to do something good for a change.

Thomas just smiled a big smile, said hello and ran back to Ray, as if meeting him was no big deal. John had to laugh to himself, "what a difference in character between the two brothers. One so serious and mature, the other totally care free."

John had always known that Margaret was a good woman, and that she had done what she had done, to survive as a widow. And he now, of course, also realised that she had done it for her boys, it must have been very hard for her. She could have chosen so many other jobs, why exactly she chose to work with the mob, he would never know.

Her husband had become a drunk after an accident at work at a butcher shop. He had managed to saw his right hand off while cutting up meat. And not paying attention to what he was doing, and if his co-worker had not been as fast to stop the bleeding and get him to a hospital, he might not have survived the accident.

Being unable to work and provide for his family, he had turned to drink. And a year later he had been found dead in the gutter, having choked on his own vomit. Thomas had only been two and Henry only five years old at the time.

John had tried to stop Margaret from being an informant, especially when he realised she was a double agent. It was bad enough working for either the mob or the police in her capacity, but both were suicide. If you got found out, you had both sides wanting your head on a plate.

It had been a dangerous game she had been playing, even worse if you had kids they could threaten you with. No wonder she had kept them a secret, which she had been able to do, as she didn't live in John's neighbourhood.

John had offered Margaret to work for him under his protection, but she had turned him down flat.

"I am not a charity case," Margaret had said. What exactly she had meant by that, he wasn't sure. Sarah had seen the look on Henry's face, when John shook his hand, and wanted to break the mood.

"What time does the service start," Sarah turned to John and asked.

"At 12.30," John replied. And as he said that the church bells started ringing, calling them to go inside. It was a beautiful church, built in the year 1697 by the Dutch settlers.

It had white walls and rows of white wooden pews, with the pulpit in the middle at the front, which had an arched window on either side. Each pew had a shelf for your hymn book and a ledge to kneel on during prayers. Anna and Ray sat down in the front middle pew with Henry and Thomas and John and Sarah sat down behind them.

The coffin was already there by the alter, with a very tasteful reef on top, consisting of white and purple flowers. The coffin was white with silver handles, very elegant. Sarah thought that John had made it all very tasteful; she had to give him credit for that.

Anna had asked Henry and Thomas if they had a message for their mother, which they would like to read during the funeral. And they had both written her a little note.

Henry had written:

I will never forget you and I will honour your name until my last breath.
Your loving son Henry xxx

Thomas had put:

Are you in heaven now?
If you are, I hope the angels
are looking after you!
Sleep tight, hope the bed bugs

don't bite.

Thomas ☺

Their messages were very typical of their characters, and made Anna, Ray, John and Sarah smile while the two of them read them out during the service.

The vicar started the funeral service with a prayer and a few chosen words about Margaret. How she had been a devoted mother and a hard working woman, taken in the prime of her life. Sarah had chosen the hymns, although she didn't know it was for that particular funeral.

Luckily, she had kept it light for the boy's sake. How great thou art to begin with, Lord of all hopefulness in the middle and ended it with Amazing Grace. It was Sarah's turn to say a few words, and she had chosen her words very carefully for Henry's and Thomas's sake.

"Margaret was a kind and gentle woman, who worked hard to keep her family together. She was very well thought of in her neighbourhood, which was clear from all the people who were always ready to support her. I shall miss her. May she rest in peace."

Sarah sat back down and was surprised to find John getting up to say a few words.

"Margaret, you were a good and loyal friend, and I always wish I could have done more for you. Your two boys Henry and Thomas are a credit to you. May you rest in peace, knowing everything will be taken care of down here."

Sarah was moved, because unless John was the best actor on the planet, that speech had come straight from the heart. She smiled warmly at him as he sat back down, and that smile meant more to John in that moment, than anything else on the planet.

The last prayers had been said, and Amazing Grace had just finished playing, when the church bells signified the end of the service. John had arranged for all of them to have lunch in a local restaurant after the service.

He had checked with Anna what the boys liked to eat, so they didn't have to sit and pretend to like something just to be polite. He just didn't want anything that could ruin the day, especially not for Henry and Thomas.

This day was for the two boys, for them to see their mother having a decent send off. Something for them to look back on as a lasting memory, and think that at least her funeral was peaceful. They were given a small cove at the back of the restaurant, away from the lunch rush. And for a quiet little town, they were very busy at that time of day.

Henry and Thomas tucked in as soon as the food arrived, really enjoying this special treat. It was homemade beef stew with bread and vegetables on the side. They were also given a glass of homemade lemonade each with the option of as many refills as they would like, which they both happily accepted.

Anna, Ray, John and Sarah shared a couple of bottles of red wine between themselves, and enjoyed the stew too. And to round it all off, they had homemade brownies with homemade vanilla ice cream. The conversation had been mainly small talk between the adults.

Anna and Ray had not known Margaret so couldn't talk about her. And Sarah and John were staying off the subject, in case they said something they didn't want the boys to know. And then Thomas asked the question everyone was wondering the answer to.

"Are we staying with Anna and Ray for good now, or are we going back to the city?" All four adults looked at each other awkwardly, not sure which one of them should take the lead.

Then John spoke, "That is a very good and important question Thomas. Well done for bringing it up."

Sarah looked at John, "That man never ceases to surprise me. He so often knew the right thing to say and putting people at ease," she had noticed on this trip. And he had a way with children that she didn't know about too.

"Do you think you boys could go out and play for a little while, so we can discuss that? But first of all, is that an arrangement the two of you would like, to live with Anna and Ray from now on?" It was still John doing all the talking.

"I will go wherever you think is best, as long as you don't separate me and my brother," Henry answered.

"I would like to live with Anna and Ray, it is much more fun than living in the city." Thomas said with his big cute smile.

Then he took Henry's hand and pulled it, "Come on, let's go and play. I saw a small green across the street, and I have got my ball in my pocket."

Henry cracked a smile for the first time that day and said, "Come on you, but don't think I will let you win," he chuckled, and off they went chatting away. Anna, Ray, John and Sarah all had smiles on their faces, after witnessing the scene of affection and banter between the two brothers that had just taken place.

117

John spoke again, "As far as I know they have no relatives in this country, as both Margaret and her husband were immigrants who came to the US alone after they were married."

After a short pause he asked, "So how do you both feel about carrying on looking after Henry and Thomas?" Directing the question at Anna and Ray.

"We would be very happy to take charge of the boys, but there are conditions," Ray answered.

"Okay, fire away," John replied.

"If we take on being Henry and Thomas's guardians," as he mentioned their names, Ray got really emotional and Sarah and John felt how much Ray cared for the boys already, "we want it to be permanently, and a legally sound arrangement."

"That is not a problem, I can easily arrange that," John replied and added, "and it is very kind and generous of you two to do it," he said looking at Anna and Ray.

Then turning to Sarah he said, "I would also like to check with you Sarah, if you are okay with such an arrangement?"

"I will be absolutely delighted if it can be arranged that way, as I know the boys will be in the best possible hands. And I know this could be a dream come true for you both," Sarah replied looking at Anna and Ray rather than John.

Then Ray spoke again, he was a down to earth straight talking man who didn't mince his words.

"Pardon me for saying this to you Mr O'Connor. I do know what kind of business you are in and I want to make sure that the papers you will arrange for us, being the guardians with the prospect of adoption of Henry and Thomas, are on the right side of the law. Can you guarantee that is what I am asking? Those boys have been through enough, and I want to make sure with, God willing, that I have the right to call them ours. And from this day forward, they are taken care of until my dying day. And also that Anna doesn't form attachments, only to have her heart broken later on, down the line."

John went bright red being spoken to in such a direct manner from such a decent man. Sarah actually felt sorry for John for a moment, but John recovered quickly.

"You have my word Mr Ray Cunningham, that the papers I will have prepared for your guardianship and possible adoption of Henry and Thomas will be one hundred per cent on the right side of the law."

"Thank you, I can see it in your eyes that you are speaking the truth, and that you are a good man," Ray replied, and sank back into his seat, with a huge look of relief on his face. Then he grabbed his wife's hand reassuringly, and Anna kissed him on the cheek, giving him a look of love and admiration.

"If you will let me, I would like to set up a trust fund for both Henry and Thomas, for their education and future," John said next in the conversation.

"Absolutely not, I am a proud man Mr O'Connor, and I will provide for my own. Anna and I had always hoped we would be blessed with children of our own, and I have put aside money on a regular basis for their future, if they should come. And now that God has given me that chance to be a father, I am prepared. Those two boys will be well taken care of, as if they were my own flesh and blood."

"Ray was a man of so much conviction, it was hard to argue with him," John thought and replied, "I respect that Mr Cunningham and as a friend of Margaret, I am taking on being an uncle to Henry and Thomas. So I would like your blessing in putting aside some money, as a contribution to those two boys. Please let me do that, not because I don't believe you cannot provide for them, but because I would like to contribute to their lives too. And as you have already pointed out, my business is no place to bring up children, if not, I would have adopted them myself. I feel I failed their mother in life, and I am not prepared to fail her in death."

John spoke it in a manner that showed so much respect for Ray and with so much honesty, that Ray said, "Okay Mr O'Connor, but I will only allow it, if they cannot touch the money until they become of age. And they will only have access to the money with yours or mine or both of ours consent."

Ray did not feel insulted by what John had said about wanting to adopt the boys himself, in different circumstances, he understood John completely.

"Absolutely! And if neither of us is alive when that time comes, they will have to have Anna's and Sarah's consent. And please call me John."

"Okay John, you have yourself an agreement, and you can call me Ray."

"I am glad we could agree on all of this, because I really want a great future for Margaret's boys. And ladies," John looked at Anna and Sarah, "Do we have your blessings in all of this?"

"Indeed you have," Anna said with a happy smile.

"Yes absolutely! As long as Anna and Ray are happy, I am happy. I am so glad that this has been agreed, and that the future of Henry and Thomas, those two lovely very young men, has been taken care of. We can never bring their mother back, but at least we have been able to give them a loving, caring and stable home," Sarah was moved to tears as she spoke, and she gave her sister and brother in law a big hug each.

Anna and Sarah were very different in appearance, but very similar in character. They were gentle, kind and strong women. Sarah was tall slim and blonde with green eyes taking after her father, while Anna only slightly shorter with dark hair and brown eyes and slightly fuller figure, taking after her mother.

Anna had met Ray on a trip to the country side when she was sixteen, while Anna was holidaying with her parents and her sister Sarah. Ray had been five years older, which at the time had not been appreciated by Anna and Sara's parents. Anna had shown no interest in Ray at all; Ray on the other hand, had not been able to take his eyes off Anna.

He knew she was young but he had also known she was the woman for him. How he knew he couldn't explain, he just knew. Anna, Sarah and their parents had been staying in Catskill, the nearest town to Ray's parent's farm, where Ray worked alongside his father. And the sister's had been invited to come and have a look at the animals on Ray's parent's farm.

Ray had been on the front porch of the main house when the sister's had arrived, and the moment he had clapped eyes on Anna, everything had changed for him. Something had opened up in him, which had never been there before. A desire to belong to someone, a desire to protect someone.

Obviously, the physical desire had been there too, but that wasn't new. Sure, he had seen nice girls before and had had physical desires, but seeing Anna for the first time had been way beyond all of that.

Ray's father had come out and looked towards the sister's and said with a sigh, "I guess I am going to have to show them around!"

Ray had jumped up from his seat and had said, "Don't worry father, I will do it." At the time, his father had not noticed Ray's eagerness, but just accepted the offer with a sigh of relief. Ray had wished that he hadn't been in his work clothes, but it could not be helped. He would have looked a bit strange if he had gone off to change, and after all, he was a farmer, nothing could change that.

"Hello young ladies, would you like to take a look around the farm?" Ray asked as he approached Anna and Sarah. Anna was the shy one, and she looked down waiting for Sarah to answer him. Sarah was two years younger than Anna, but had a lot more confidence.

"Yes I thought that was why we are here, to look around?" Sarah said with a lot of attitude and more confidence than she felt. Ray went bright red and as he was a paled skinned man, it was very obvious.

Sarah had noticed that Ray could not take his eyes off Anna and she felt invisible, so she retaliated with a bad attitude. She also got fed up with Anna's shyness and having to take charge all the time.

Anna had looked up as Sarah had spoken, and had felt that her sister had been a little bit rude in her approach. And when she had seen Ray turning bright red in embarrassment, it had made her feel a little bit sorry for him.

So to break the ice she had asked shyly, "What kind of animals have you got on your farm?" Ray gave her a big smile and said, "We have cows, a few sheep, a lot of chickens, a couple of horses, two dogs and four cats. Which animals would you like to see first?"

As he asked, a beautiful white cat came strolling towards them, and Anna immediately crouched down to stroke it. And it had put a big smile on her face.

"So you are an animal lover then?" Ray asked grinning from ear to ear.

"Yes she is, I can't get her away from them," Sarah replied on Anna's behalf. Sarah had done that a lot back then, as Anna rarely answered questions, but had just used to look down shyly most of the time. Sarah was already bored, she had not really been into animals, and she had preferred good old nature, people and books.

She had wished she could have left them to it and head to a cosy place where she could read her book. She had wanted to suggest that, as Ray had looked harmless enough and her parents would never have needed to know.

"Why don't you two animal lovers go off and look at the animals, and you can maybe show me a nice spot in the shade somewhere where I can read my book?" Sarah had suggested, having directed the question towards Ray. Anna had looked at Sarah in shock.

"What was she thinking? Had she gone mad? I don't want to be left alone with this man," Anna had thought to herself, although she had wanted to say it out loud she hadn't as she didn't want to be rude.

Ray had saved the day by saying, "I think it is better if we all stick together." He had caught the look on Anna's face, and had not wanted to put her in a situation she was not comfortable with. However, he would have loved to have her to himself, to have gotten to know her a little.

"Okay, show us the furry things then," Sarah had said resigned to the fact that she was going to play gooseberry to Anna and Ray, looking at things she had no interest in. Ray had teased Sarah about that incident at the lunch table after Margaret's funeral, and Sarah had teased him about how besotted he had been about Anna.

The three of them had known each other a long time, and there was a lot of love and friendship between them. John was enjoying the banter between the three of them too.

"So what happened next?" John asked. "Well Sarah spent the rest of the day making it really clear she was bored and not interested in anything I was showing them," Ray answered.

John looked at Sarah in surprise, "Wow, that is not the Sarah I have gotten to know," John said. Sarah smiled confidently and said, "It was a long time ago, and I was a stroppy teenager, who didn't want to spend a whole day of my holiday on a farm."

John smiled at the comment and Ray carried on and said, "Anna on the other hand was excited about everything I showed her. From sheep to cows to chickens even the barns, but most of all she loved the horses," Ray said and laughed, "which gave me an opportunity to get to know her a little and for her to be comfortable around me. And of course, the thought struck me that she was the perfect farmer's wife material."

The last sentence he said with a very cheeky look on his face smiling lovingly at Anna. And Anna looked lovingly back at him also remembering that first day, when she had been completely oblivious to his affections.

Then Ray slipped into his own thoughts, while the others talked amongst themselves. It had been such a pleasure to spend the day with Anna that first time. It had stayed with him ever since. And he had tried to work out how he could possibly get to see her again, while she was in the area. And secondly, how it could be possible to stay in touch with her, without anyone thinking he was a cradle snatcher.

Then he had come up with this brilliant idea that he could suggest that Anna could write and ask about the animals and life on the farm after she had returned to the city. He had not suggested it straight away; the opportunity had come a few days later.

Sarah had thought that Ray was ancient, but could see that he had the right temperament for Anna. A calm and decent man, who would love and respect her.

Sarah hadn't been interested in boys yet; she had wanted independence and a life of her own. Where she could do what she wanted, when she wanted.

She had been very mature for her age and saw the women around her as slaves to their homes and husbands. She had not had those childlike qualities that Anna had had at that age, although she was younger than Anna.

She developed those childlike wonders later in life, as John had discovered up at his cabin. That's why, he had been so surprised at Ray's story, as she didn't sound like the Sarah he knew. Later that summer, when they had returned from their holiday, Sarah had met Charlie and fell in love herself.

Chapter Fourteen

Sarah had seen spirits and communicated with them since she was a child, and the spirits had always been guiding and teaching her. She had instinctively never mentioned it to anyone, because she had felt that they would not have understood. She had only ever spoken to one person about it, and that had been a little old lady who had lived on their street.

The lady's name had been Mrs Williams, and she had read people's tea leaves. The people in their neighbourhood had claimed that it had been a lot of nonsense, but secretly most of them had gone to see her for "a cup of tea." And had casually asked her if she saw anything in their tea leaves in the bottom of their empty tea cups, simply to hear what "nonsense" Mrs Williams would come up with.

Of course no one had ever given her credit for being right, but Mrs Williams had not cared. Mrs Williams had had a lot of time for Sarah, as she knew what she had been dealing with.

Mrs Williams had seen all the spirits "hanging" around Sarah all the time trying to get through and communicate with her. And she had been very impressed with the way Sarah had taken it all in her stride, having organised the spirits so they didn't all came through at the same time, potentially driving her crazy.

Sarah had demanded of the spirits to respect her wishes, and had understood that she had a "door keeper" who would protect her from overload, if she gave clear instructions to the door keeper. (A door keeper in the psychic sense is a spirit who mediums use to open and close the door to the spirit world, to one or more than one spirit(s) at any time.

So that the medium can "hear", "sense", or "see" what is being communicated.) Mrs Williams and Sarah used to talk for hours, about the spirit world, spirit behaviour and spirit communication. There was nothing Sarah had loved more than those hours she had spent regularly with Mrs Williams. And neither of them had ever spoken to anyone else about their talks.

Not because it had been a secret, but because to them it had been something sacred. When the tour of the farm had been over, Ray's mother had invited the sisters to have some homemade lemonade on the veranda of the main house. Anna and Sarah had gratefully accepted, as by then they were hot and very thirsty.

It had been a very hot day, and they had been out in the direct sunlight for a lot of it. Thankfully, their mother had insisted they wore wide brimmed sun hats and a light scarfs around their shoulders, to protect them against the strong sun. When they had run out of animals to look at, Anna and Ray both had gone very shy and quiet.

Ray's mother had noticed that he had been smitten with Anna, and had hoped that he would keep it under wraps as the girl had been very young. Ray's mother had been doing most of the talking; having asked the sister's what they had planned for the rest of their holiday. And had told them that they were very welcome to come back to the farm again.

When she had said that, Anna's face had lit up, and so had Ray's, but Sarah had looked like she would have rather done anything else than come back again. Ray's mother had smiled to herself and she had thought, "The two sisters could not be more different than if they had come from two different families."

When the sisters had left the farm having been picked up by their father, Sarah knew that Anna and Ray would end up together.

She had seen their wedding very clearly, in her mind's eye. But she had not told her sister that, until after her and Ray had been married as people always had to make their choices in life, regardless of what spirit said. And Anna might have cut off all contact, as in that moment in time she was not interested in Ray.

What was true today, or right today, could be changed tomorrow. Sarah would come back to the farm with Anna, if she had to, as she did not want to let her sister down. If that was Anna's destiny, then she had wanted to be part of it and support it from the beginning.

Anna had gone back to the farm twice within a few days of the first visit, and it had always been arranged in advance. Both times Ray's had had errands in town and had bumped into the sisters and their parents.

The first time in the ice cream parlour one late afternoon, where Anna and Sarah were having ice cream and their parents Walter and Elizabeth were having coffee. Ray's face had lit up when he saw them and Walter had gestured for him to join them.

"Let me buy you a coffee to say thank you for showing our girls around the farm the other day," Walter had said.

"Oh you don't have to do that sir, it was an absolute pleasure," when Ray had said that, Anna had blushed and Sarah had thought cheekily to herself, "I bet it was," and smiled.

"I insist," Walter had said.

"Okay, just a quick coffee then," Ray had answered.

"Squeeze in next to the girls," Walter had commanded. Sarah had been sitting in the aisle seat of the booth, which her mother had been very pleased about.

"Sarah can handle herself, even if she is the youngest, but Anna can't, she always need her sisters back up," she had thought to herself.

It had been obvious to Elizabeth that Ray was sweet on her Anna, "And the boy must be at least twenty," she had thought.

Ray had started to tell Anna about the animals and how they were doing, and had said that she was welcome to come and visit again any time.

"You too Sarah, although I am not sure you enjoyed it that much," he had said and laughed.

"Well let's put it this way, that wasn't my favourite day of our vacation so far," Sarah replied.

"Sarah, don't be so rude," her mother had reprimanded her.

"Oh Ray can take it, he's a big boy, and our Sarah will say it as it is, and I like that," Walter had said looking lovingly at his youngest daughter.

He had always been able to relate to Sarah as she was very straight forward and said as it was. Anna in their father's opinion had been more difficult for him to relate to as she had been very shy and awkward, especially around men.

Ray had not taken offence at Sarah's comment, he had found it funny. And it had not been a surprise to him; he had already known that Sarah had been bored that day on the farm. If it had been Anna having those opinions, he probably would have felt a bit upset.

"Can I go again daddy?" Anna had asked, "even if Sarah doesn't want to come, please."

"You can't go out there on your own darling," her mother had said and Anna had looked very disappointed.

Ray had sensed Elizabeth's concern and had immediately said, "It was just a suggestion, and maybe instead you could write from time to time asking about the animals, and I will write back with an update."

"Okay, Anna had said and looked down with disappointment on her face. Walter had sensed that there was something weird going on, but had not worked out what it was.

But he had rescued the whole situation by having said, "I'll tell you what, my sweet Anna, I will take you out to the farm one day that suits Ray, I'm sure your mother and Sarah can think of something to do without us. I wouldn't mind seeing the farm myself, how's that?"

He had asked and looked at Anna with a gentle smile on his face. He hadn't often gotten through to Anna, and he hated it when she withdrew like she had done in that situation.

Anna's face lit up, "Will you daddy? I would love that, and then I can show you the lambs and the kittens."

"That's settled then, what day will work for you Ray? We don't want to get in your way." Walter had said.

"Oh any day, as long as you give me advanced warning," Ray had replied.

"Okay, which day do you and Sarah want to do your own thing Elizabeth," he asked his wife. She had been tempted to say let's all stay together instead of splitting up, as she had not been sure what Walter had been playing at. Her thought had been that, "men can be so thick sometimes."

She had decided to have a quiet word with her husband later on. But all she said was, "Oh any day darling, you choose," with a sweet smile.

Walter had looked at her with suspicion, "What is going on with Elizabeth, she is acting strange?" had been his thoughts.

"Okay Ray, the ball is in your court, you get to name the day," Walter had said.

"Thursday is good, gives me a chance to warn the animals that you are coming," Ray had replied with a happy, cheeky look on his face, having glanced over at Anna.

Walter had laughed out loud, "A farmer with a sense of humour, I love it." Anna had looked down shyly again, this time she had a happy smile on her face. Ray had not wanted to overstay his welcome, so had made his excuses and left as soon as they had made the arrangements.

Sarah had noticed her mother's concern regarding Ray, and had wanted to put her at ease and had said, "He seems to be a decent man, that Ray, don't you think?"

"I guess, as long as he stays away from your sister, he is definitely sweet on her!" her mother had said and had turned her nose up in the air as women do with that look, "Mark my word."

"Oh mother, don't be so mellow dramatic. So he thinks Anna is pretty, who wouldn't? And he finds it hard to take his eyes off her, but he wouldn't do anything stupid, and you know that. And daddy will be there, and you know that if any man stepped out of line, daddy would come down on him like a ton of bricks."

Sarah had really gone for it; she had believed that Anna and Ray had to get a chance to get to know each other a little.

Her mother had looked at her, really studied her and had said, "How did you get to be so wise, my dear Sarah? I think you spend too much time at Mrs Williams's house." It had been Sarah's turn to study her mother.

She had wondered, "How does she know? Nothing gets past my mother!" Sarah had never told her mother she was going to see Mrs Williams, but still she had known. She was guessing mothers had a sixth sense when it came to their children, to keep them from harm.

"So you think Mrs Williams is wise?" Sarah had asked her mother.

"Well, for someone so "loopy" she seems to get an awful lot right in her predictions. And not only that, she tends to give people very good advice, to go with her predictions. So if you have a gift like she has, you should definitely carry on learning from her," her mother had said.

Sarah had been absolutely astonished, "Her mother had known about her psychic abilities all along, and had never said anything?"

"Don't be put off by what I just said about Mrs Williams dear, if that is your path, then I am glad you have a kind, generous and powerful mentor. And you don't have to tell me anything about it," had been her mother's final words about the subject.

Sarah had been floored, literally, and sat down on the nearest bench, to take it all in. For years to come after that, she had remembered that conversation with her mother, and had never seen her in the same light again.

In that moment, her mother had become another amazing and wise woman in her life, and as a result of it, they had also become much closer.

Before that conversation her mother had occurred to her as a bit bossy with all of them, including her father. But after the conversation, she had been able to see that her mother saw everything, and was being protective and loving in her own way.

Elizabeth had decided not to mention to her husband, that Ray was sweet on Anna. She was a wise woman, and having thought about what Sarah had said and her own words to Sarah, she had come to the conclusion that if this was part of Anna's path, she should let it unfold naturally. And like Sarah so wisely had said, Walter would be there, nothing untoward could happen.

Also, Ray's family had a very good reputation in the area; surely he was not going to risk spoiling that. And he really had not come across as a sleazy type. Walter had meant to ask his wife about her strange behaviour in the ice cream parlour that day, but luckily had forgotten all about it, as she had already decided not to tell him about Ray's infatuation.

Thursday had come and Sarah had been excited about some alone time with her mother, and Anna had been delighted about going back to the farm. Walter had not been particularly interested in the farm or any farm for that matter, but Anna had been very shy and had hardly ever expressed an interest in anything, so he had felt that it would be good for her to go again.

And Ray had seemed to know how to handle her, so as far as he had been concerned it had all been good. And poor Sarah had always been lumbered with her sister and her shy ways, so he had felt that he had some time while they were on vacation, it was his turn to look out for Anna.

Ray had known that the second visit had to be all about the farm. How it was run, how they dealt with the animals and who did what. He had known that he had to build up a friendship with Anna's father as well as with Anna, for him to have a chance to let it develop into something with a possible future.

When Walter had seen Anna in the farm environment, he had been surprised to see her blossom beyond belief. She had obviously been meant for country life, not the city. And as the day had passed, he had seen the special interest Ray had showed Anna, however much Ray had tried to hide it.

By the end of the day, Walter had decided to encourage the friendship. Of course he knew that Anna had still been very young, and he would keep an eye on her, to see if over time she started to show an interest in Ray. It had been the start of a great friendship between Anna and Ray, they had so much in common, and Ray could not have asked for a better partnership, when that time had come.

For the next two years they wrote to each other, and Anna went to stay on the farm on numerous occasions. What for Anna had been a pure friendship had eventually turned romantic. When she had turned eighteen, and had suddenly felt she could no longer imagine her life without Ray in it.

One day, Anna had stood on the farm, looking at Ray who was taking care of one of the horses, and she had known she was in love with him. And that evening, after Ray had felt encouraged by the look in Anna's eyes, when she had looked straight at him, he had kissed her on the veranda.

It had been an intense kiss, full of love and passion for both of them. Not long after, Ray had asked Anna to marry him, and she had happily accepted. Both families had been extremely happy with the union, and within just a few months, they were married in a beautiful ceremony.

Anna had never been so happy in her life, she absolutely loved being Ray's wife and living on the farm. They had been very happy and they still were, but there had been sadness for both of them that they had never managed to conceive a child together. They had both wanted a farm full of their children.

So when Sarah in her desperation, had called in the early morning after Margaret had died, and asked if they could look after Henry and Thomas for a while, they had both been delighted. And making the arrangement they had just done with John, was a dream come through for both Anna and Ray.

Sarah went outside to call the boys back into the restaurant, Anna was too emotional to do it. She didn't want the boys to see that she was crying, even though it was happy tears. She was worried they should think she was upset. John paid the bill and told them they were all going back to the churchyard to say a final farewell to Margaret.

He had organised so that Margaret would be buried while they were having lunch, and had decided that it might be too much for the two young boys, to watch their mother be put in the ground. They all walked slowly back to the Old Dutch Church, and this time both Henry and Thomas were a little apprehensive, as they didn't know what to expect.

Anna and Ray had talked them through the funeral, but not what happens at a graveside. Margaret's grave had been covered with dirt, and a small wooden cross had been put up with a plaque, saying Margaret Wilson, and all the beautiful flowers had been placed on top of the grave.

They all stopped at the foot end for a little while, until Thomas broke the silence.

"I want to be buried here too, next to my mum," he said quietly.

"Of course," John replied, "I will make sure that you have that option." Henry was crying, as he now felt safe to do so, and Thomas went over and stood next to him, and took his older brother's hand. It was a beautiful sight, two lovely young brothers so very different, united in grief.

Sarah reflected on the fact that she really had not known Margaret at all, but here she was connected to her forever through her sons and her own sister. Then, John addressed Henry and Thomas, "Anna and Ray will love to foster you with a view to legally adopt you as their own children, which can easily be arranged. And I want to check with you both if that it is what you want?"

Henry and Thomas looked at each other to check the other's reaction, then they both smiled, said yes, and Thomas ran and hugged Ray. Henry being more formal went and shook Ray's hand and said thank you, then gently hugged Anna and said thank you again.

John smiled a very happy and satisfied smile, as he watched the scene unfold, and thought to himself, "If I only ever get to do one thing right in my life, I believe this is it. Providing a wonderful and caring couple with children they have dreamt of for so long, and giving two orphaned boys a stable loving home."

But in reality, he knew that it was mostly Sarah's doing, he had just put the finishing touches on it all. Sarah was very moved too and had similar thoughts to John.

"If nothing else, you got this one right John," she thought to herself. John and Sarah were walking the happy "family" of four back to their truck, and on the way John wanted them to stop at his car. He opened the trunk which had four boxes in it, full of Henry and Thomas's things. And one with some of their mother's possession, things he believed the boys would treasure.

He had got a couple of his guys to go and clean out Margaret's flat, pretending to be relatives of the boys. He had also settled all bills, leaving no clues or traces.

"How very kind of you," Anna said, "Isn't it boys?"

"Yes, thank you very much," Henry said and shook John's hand with tears of appreciation in his eyes. A very different look from the first one John had got earlier that day.

Henry was already looking forward to going through his mother's things, wondering what might be in there. Thomas was all excited, shouting, "Thank you, are my toys in there?" was his main concern.

"I believe they are," John answered. Then John handed Henry a jewellery box, and inside were Margaret's wedding ring.

Henry started sobbing quietly, "You are a very kind man, Mr O'Connor." Coming from that young man who had just lost his mother almost moved John to tears too. Henry carried one of the boxes, John one, Ray one and the last one Anna and Sarah carried between them. They reached Ray's truck, and said their good byes.

Ray took John's hand and shook it firmly and said, "Thank you for everything you have done, and are about to do. Please keep us informed, and you are welcome to come and visit any time. Just don't bring the mob," Ray was smiling as his last words were a joke.

John did recognise that it was a joke and grinned his famous grin and said, "You are most welcome, it has been an absolute pleasure," and he really meant it.

"But if you ever step out of line with those boys, I will bring the mob to deal with you," he added smiling from ear to ear, knowing full well that would never happen, as Ray would never lay a hand on those boys.

Ray laughed and said, "That is fair enough, I look forward to beating up a few hooligans!" John and Sarah walked back to John's car in silence. Sarah embarrassed at her "performance" that morning back in the city, and John now very unsure of what would happen next.

"Would he ever see Sarah again, or was it over after today?"

"Would you like to go for a walk, before we set off?" He asked Sarah politely.

She suddenly felt so awkward in his company that she was dreading the drive back to the city, let alone a walk with him. But she thought for a moment and decided that a walk in the lovely weather would do her good. And hopefully, it would cool down a bit, so the drive would be more comfortable.

"Yes that sounds like a good idea," she answered rather shyly. John had noticed her hesitation, but didn't let on; he just wanted her to be comfortable in his company again. That last thought had become his theme song around Sarah, he thought to himself, with a huge amount of sadness and regret.

But all he said was, "Good," and smiled, "Let's explore a little."

They found a small path that led them through a field down to a small stream. It was peaceful and quiet and neither of them felt the need to talk. And after a while they headed back to the car, and started their journey back to the city and the unknown.

Sarah was the one who broke the silence, "What you have done for Margaret's boys and my sister and brother in law, is very kind, and I am sure Margaret is smiling down on you today. Both for making her funeral a peaceful and beautiful event, and for providing her sons with a loving stable home. And for that, I thank you. And from dreading this day, I have actually loved almost every moment of it, if I can say that about a funeral."

After hearing all that, John felt a peace come over him and confirmed to himself, what he had thought earlier, "I did at least get this right."

"Thank you for saying that Sarah, it means a lot to me. And it really was an absolute pleasure to put it all together, and for once, making a few people happy," John replied with a content smile on his face.

Sarah really could not work John out, "Is he a saint or a monster, I can't tell. He is both, there are two people in his body," she decided. They didn't speak much after that on the journey back, only the odd practical thing like restroom stops and so forth.

As John stopped the car at Sarah's drop off point, he asked her to hold on for a moment.

"I know you think I am a monster with the odd human behaviour, and I guess that's fair enough. But I would be grateful if you, at some point, will allow me to tell you my story. After that, you will never have to see me again if you choose to," John said.

Sarah replied, "I will think about it," in a serious and contemplative voice.

"That is all I can ask, thank you," John said and waved her off. After such a beautiful and in a many ways happy day, it was heart breaking to say good bye to Sarah. It was with a very heavy heart he drove home, not knowing what the future held.

Chapter Fifteen

Sarah became restless after Margaret's funeral; nothing felt the same any more. If she wanted to speak to her sister, she had to go to a public telephone. To make sure if they were still listening in on her telephone, they wouldn't find out about Margaret's boys.

She didn't feel like booking in clients either, it was as if her life in the city was over. She had always thought she was a city girl, but lately the countryside had become more and more appealing. She decided to travel up to see her sister, Ray and the boys.

She wanted to have a conversation with Anna about the possibility of selling her house in New York City and buying a small house for herself near them. She took the coach to Catskill, which was the nearest town to Ray's and Anna's farm, where they had holidayed many times with their parents, and Ray picked her up from there.

He was surprised to see Sarah so soon after the funeral, she normally only visited them two or three times a year. Usually at Christmas, in the summer and occasionally at Easter.

Ray had obviously always known that Sarah was not interested in farming of any kind, but he was guessing that she wanted to see how Henry and Thomas were settling in. It was always nice to see her and he knew Anna would be pleased, as she always enjoyed it when her sister visited.

Henry and Thomas were also excited, as they were used to having more people around than they saw on the farm. Ray and Sarah pulled up around 5pm and Anna had supper ready, as they always ate early on the farm. Because of the early start of a farmer like Ray, all meals were taken much earlier than in the city.

Ray was up at 5am to feed the animals and Anna got up at the same time too, to have breakfast ready for him when he got back to the main house. Lunch would be at 11 am and then now supper at 5pm.

Thomas came running out chatting away about what he and Ray had done that day, what they were having for supper and that there would be dessert too. He was so excited, which Sarah thought was so nice to see.

Henry stood on the veranda looking a little shy and pleased at the same time. Sarah smiled and laughed and hugged them both in turn, taking it all in. What a difference it makes with a couple of children on the farm, she had never really appreciated the farm before, but today she saw it with new eyes.

And she thought to herself, "Family is everything," and felt the pain of the loss of her beloved husband more acutely than she had for a long time. And the fact that she could have been a mother of two as well, if Charlie had lived. Anna noticed the difference in Sarah immediately, and felt concerned.

She had been so wrapped up in her own new found happiness that she had not stopped to think about how this whole Margaret business must have affected Sarah. Anna made a promise to herself that she would make sure Sarah and herself would get some alone time in the next day or so.

In the meantime, they had a fun filled noisy supper, with great homemade food and the boys for entertainment. Sarah could not remember the last time she had enjoyed herself that much.

After supper, Sarah helped Anna with the dishes, after the boys had cleared the table. Normally Henry would help with the dishes, but even he had sensed that the two sisters would like some time alone. So he joined Ray and Thomas with the evening feed and chores.

As soon as Ray and the boys were out of ear shot, Anna turned to Sarah and asked, in a gentle loving way, "Why are you really here Sarah? It's not like you to leave the city for no reason. And I am not asking because I don't want you here, you know that right?"

As soon as Anna had spoken the words, Sarah started to sob uncontrollably.

"My dear Sarah," Anna said and put her arms around her, "Come and sit down," she said as she guided Sarah to the sofa in the living room. Anna just held Sarah until her sobbing stopped and her breathing had calmed down.

"We have got about an hour before they are back, so please tell me what is bothering you, so I can help," Anna said looking lovingly at Sarah.

"I thought I had the life I wanted," Sarah started.

"But this whole business with Margaret has really shaken me up. The city does not seem so friendly and exciting any more, and I want to get away from John, and the life he leads. So I was thinking that with your blessing, I could find

135

a small house around here to buy. That way we could see a lot more of each other, when it suits you of course now that you have your hands even more full than before. What do you think?"

Sarah finished with a hopeful look in her eyes. Anna looked very surprised, and at the same time also happy.

"I would love that, but are you sure? You have always been a city girl; nothing much goes on around here."

"Nothing much apart from nature, sounds good right now," Sarah replied.

Anna looked concerned now, "I know that the death of Margaret Wilson, the boy's mother and the way you ended up being involved has upset you, and has also been traumatic for you, but things will get back to normal Sarah. I would love to have you near, you can even live with us here on the farm if you want to, but you have to make sure it is absolutely the right thing for you. And whatever you decide, I will support you one hundred per cent.

"Regarding John I am a little bit bewildered. Surely after the funeral was over you don't have to have anything to do with him again, unless you wish to?" Anna finished.

"It's complicated Anna, and I feel like such a fool. I thought that John was an arrogant, full of himself jerk from the mob. Then I got to know him, a kind and generous man with real human qualities. But I couldn't get it out of my head that he might have been behind the killing of Margaret, from something she told me when we were waiting for the ambulance."

At this point Anna looked really shocked, but Sarah carried on.

"But then this young man turned up on my door step, and confessed to having run Margaret over and dumped her on my door step. And in the meantime, the mob was going crazy, wondering who had bumped her off. And I thought it served them all right, so I haven't told a soul until now. So you see, it is really confusing. Who is he? He has also been hinting at, that he wanted to help Margaret, and he has been begging me to tell me his life story, to explain himself. What is there to explain?" Sarah shouted, "He is part of the mob, what is there to explain?"

Anna felt there was more to it than all that, and asked, "Why are you so upset about him, when all you have to do, is walk away?"

"Because he is the first man I have even remotely liked since Charlie died, and I think he likes me too. But I cannot be with a man like that, I just cannot," Sarah was more talking to herself now, shaking her head gently. Anna felt

Sarah's pain and understood her concerns, but before she could say anything Sarah continued.

"I don't know for sure if he likes me, or maybe he was just keeping me sweet, wondering how much I know. And even if he does like me, I cannot settle for a man like that. So you see, either way I have to get away."

"I see, but you could just hear him out, before you say good bye for good, to get some kind of closure. Unless," Anna hesitated and for a moment she felt a bit of panic, "you fear for your life Sarah? Do you think we should all fear for our lives," Anna asked, feeling the panic rising.

Sarah looked at her and said, "Oh my god, I hadn't thought of that," and for a moment they were both panicking.

Anna was quick thinking, "You must tell John about the young man who confessed, so that he knows, that you know, he didn't kill Margaret. That way we will all be safe, and what he chooses to do with that young man, is up to him."

Sarah looked at Anna with admiration, "Yes you are right, that is a good plan of action. I will even let him tell me his life story if it makes him feel better and makes him leave me alone. Good, now that we know what we are doing, let's finish those dishes," Sarah said and smiled at Anna as they both got off the sofa.

The next couple of days, Sarah helped Anna out in the house. While Henry carried on doing farm chores wit Ray and Thomas, and found that he quite liked the physical work. It helped with letting off steam, around his anger and frustration over his mother's death.

Although he missed the female company of Anna, but was sure as soon as Sarah left, he could go back to doing some chores in the house with Anna again. Anna and Sarah also went for long walks, talking about the past, their parents, and occasionally Charlie, but Anna could see that that was still a very sore subject.

She was beginning to feel Sarah's loneliness, which made her feel guilty, now that she had found such complete happiness. She hoped in time that Sarah would find happiness again, she didn't wish for her to be alone for the rest of her life.

While on their walks, they had been picking berries to make pies with. Anna was a natural farmer's wife, who cooked the most wholesome delicious food, which Henry and Thomas in particular enjoyed tremendously. On the third evening, the telephone rang and it was John wanting to speak to Ray.

"Hi John, what can I do for you?" Ray asked.

"I have got the initial paperwork ready from my attorney, regarding you and Anna fostering Henry and Thomas, and I can bring them to you to sign," John said.

"That's great, yes anytime that is good for you works for me. We are always here, as you know," Ray replied.

"How about tomorrow?" John asked.

"Yeah, tomorrow is good; just make sure you are here in plenty of time for supper at 5pm. I don't want you to miss Anna's wonderful food," he said and smiled.

"And of course, you must stay the night, don't want you to do a whole round trip in one day."

"Great, I will be there well before supper. And if you are busy I will go for a walk, or hang out with Henry and Thomas. And you don't have to give me a bed for the night; I don't want to inconvenience you. I know that on a farm, there are things to do around the clock. I am sure I can find a room somewhere nearby," John said.

"I wouldn't dream of it; you are staying with us. And if we are all busy, Sarah can keep you company," Ray replied.

"Sarah? John got all butterflies in his stomach.

"She is up there with you?" He was trying to keep his voice casual.

"Yeah, she has been here for a couple of days now," Ray replied, "so we shall see you tomorrow John, bye," Ray said and hung up.

When Ray came back into the living room, Anna asked, "Who was that, Ray?"

"Oh that was John; he has got the initial paperwork ready for us to sign. So he is coming up tomorrow, and I invited him to stay the night. You don't mind, do you? It is very generous of him to bring them, as he could have insisted on us going all the way down to the city to sign. He is a decent man, really," Ray said.

Anna kept her posture and replied, "Of course, Ray, that is okay, can't expect him to do the round trip in one day." She glanced over at Sarah.

"Good," Ray said and started engaging in a card game with the boys.

"Sorry," Anna whispered to Sarah.

"It's okay; it's actually good in a way, as this will give me an opportunity to have the conversation with him, in a safe environment, and not on my own. I am sure it will be fine, now that I have calmed down," Sarah said, but she was nervous about seeing John again.

She was worried she would still have feelings for him, and get sucked into some kind of sob story. Why she thought that she didn't know, maybe because he had begged her so many times to tell his story. But at least she was in a safe place, and not on his turf for a change.

When John came off the telephone, he felt nervous and delighted at the same time. At least he would get to see Sarah again, and maybe even get to spend some time alone with her.

Suddenly, he felt excited about the next day, instead of feeling bored about having to drive all the way up there. He had been looking forwards to seeing Henry and Thomas again, though.

John arrived just after 3pm, and Anna was the only one who was around to greet him. She had just started to prepare the vegetables for supper, and was trying to act normal, as her conversation with Sarah had made her worried.

She felt uneasy and she now knew what Sarah meant by John having two personalities, one polite and generous one, the other one they could only guess. As Sarah, she could not understand why and how John had ended up in the mob. But she truly felt that the essence of John was good, and she had no reasonable explanation for that.

John offered to help Anna preparing supper, and she accepted gracefully, to keep him occupied. Instead of having to entertain him while she was busy, thinking he would be useless. But she was very pleasantly surprised, how good John was in the kitchen.

Sarah had gone for a walk to clear her head and think about how she wanted to approach the conversation with John. And when she got back to the house, she could hear laughter in the kitchen, and went to have a look.

She found Anna and John chatting away, while chopping vegetables.

"Hello," she said quietly, and felt very uncomfortable. It was as if John had infiltrated her family, and stolen her ally.

John immediately spotted the look of discomfort on Sarah's face, and tried to neutralise the situation by saying, "I thought I should earn my food by helping Anna, and you know how much I like to cook."

Anna had noticed the look on her Sarah's face too, and felt very bad that she had made her sister feel uncomfortable.

"Did you have a nice walk?" Anna asked Sarah.

"Yes, thank you, it was good," Sarah replied.

"I tell you what, why don't the two of you go and sit on the veranda with a cold drink, and I will finish getting supper ready. Anna has told me what she is making, and I know what to do," John said in the hope that that would make Sarah feel better. Anna looked to Sarah for a yes or a no.

Sarah said "Yes," and immediately went out on to the veranda.

Anna put on her bossy voice and said, "Okay John, you know what to do, and I trust you to make it edible, we have high standards in this house. I will get Sarah and myself some nice cold lemonade and join her on the veranda."

"Aye, aye captain," John said and saluted. When Anna entered the veranda, Sarah was deep in thought wishing her feelings about the scene in the kitchen had not been so obvious.

She wanted to have the upper hand when speaking to John, hopefully later on that day. But she would probably never have the upper hand with John; he was just too good a manipulator.

Anna sat down with the two glasses of lemonade and said, "I am sorry, I didn't know what to do with him when he arrived. And when he offered to help, it meant I didn't have to entertain him until the rest of you showed up. And I was just so pleased that he wasn't getting in the way, but actually knew what he was doing."

"You don't have to apologise; it was me being silly. I thought you were chatting with one of your neighbours, and got taken by surprise, that's all. I am fine, really." Sarah said with a reassuring look at her sister.

"Okay, I believe you, and don't worry, I think your conversation with him will be just fine," Anna replied.

Ray, Henry and Thomas returned from their chores at 4.45pm, to clean up before supper, and they were all pleased to see John. Anna and Sarah were setting the table, and John was putting the final touches on supper.

They were having homemade chicken soup and fresh homemade bread, which Anna had baked that morning. Everybody was enjoying the supper and John was complimenting Anna on her bread.

"This is one of the best bread I have ever tasted, but don't tell Rose, it would only upset her. She thinks that nobody can feed me better, more enjoyable food than her," John said and laughed.

The boys laughed too and Thomas asked, "who is Rose, is she your wife?"

"No, she is my housekeeper," John answered slightly embarrassed by the question.

"You have a house keeper?" Thomas asked wide eyed.

"I do," John answered and smiled.

"So how come you cook then, I thought the housekeeper would do that?" Thomas carried on the interrogation.

"Yes she does, and she doesn't know that I cook. I discovered that I enjoy cooking, when I was up at my cabin, and it really relaxes me. So will you keep my secret?" John asked Thomas.

"Cool, and yes I will keep your secret from Rose that is, because everybody around this table now knows."

Everybody around the table laughed at that last line.

"Anna, can I learn to cook, will you teach me?" Thomas asked with enthusiasm.

"Yes of course, you are more than welcome to learn. Your brother has already started to take an interest, so soon, I can have weekends off from cooking, right boys?" Anna said looking at them both smiling.

"Absolutely," Henry and Thomas said in unison, and Henry added, "If you think we will get that good it will be a pleasure."

"Do you see what you have started, John? Soon I will have no one to help me with the animals and the fields, but at least I will have plenty of inedible food to eat," Ray said with a big smile on his face, and winked at the boys.

Thomas looked a little bit upset and said, "I will still help you Ray, I won't let you down, I can do both you know."

"Don't upset yourself Thomas, I was only joking. You can do whatever you want with your days until you go back to school. We don't run a child labour camp here."

Ray replied smiling gently at Thomas. John was grinning from ear to ear, "Watch out Anna, you might soon be free from your cooking duties," John said looking at Anna.

Anna smiled, "Oh I don't mind, I would then be able to do a little bit of painting from time to time maybe. And the most important thing is for Henry and Thomas to be happy here," she said looking lovingly at her two boys.

Henry and Thomas had not been with them very long, but she already loved them dearly.

"Why do you always say Henry's name before mine. Is he more important than me?" Thomas asked out of the blue with a concerned look on his face. The adults around the table had to stop themselves from laughing not to upset Thomas, and Ray was the first one to come up with an answer.

"No Thomas, he is not more important than you, nor are you more important than him. It is just the norm to mention children in order of their age from the eldest to the youngest, but if that concerns you, we can mix it up. Sometime starting with your name and sometimes with Henry's, is that okay?" Ray asked looking at Thomas.

"Only if it is okay with Henry," Thomas said looking at his brother.

Henry smiled and said, "They can call out your name first every time, if that makes you happy, Thomas. It makes no difference to me, I know I am older, nothing can change that." The adults were moved by the loving concern Henry always had for his brother.

"Cool, but we will do it Ray's way, it's only fair," Thomas replied to his brother with a big smile, and gave Ray an admiring look.

John turned to Anna and said, "After witnessing you all here today, I have no doubt that Thomas and Henry are already very happy here with you. Am I right boys?" he asked looking at Henry and Thomas.

"Yes," they both answered again in unison, both smiling at Anna and Ray.

"So let's get the papers signed, to make this a more permanent arrangement," John said.

"Okay, let's clear the table and we can have dessert on the veranda with our coffee," Anna responded. They all helped to clear the table and Sarah went to set the veranda table, ready for dessert. They didn't always have dessert after supper on week nights, but Anna had made apple pie with custard, as they had two guests that evening.

The signing of the papers felt very ceremonious for all of them, and Anna hugged Henry and Thomas intensely and Ray shook John's hand.

Sarah's thoughts went to Margaret for a moment, hoping she was able to see this moment, and feel that her boys were safe and well taken care of. She herself felt satisfied that she had kept her promise to Margaret that she had made on that terrible night.

She was very happy for her sister Anna, and at the same time, very sad for Margaret. After dessert and paper signing, Anna and the boys cleared the table. Ray went to check on the animals and the boys joined him, as Anna had insisted on doing the dishes herself.

So it was just Sarah and John left at the table, the way Anna had hoped.

"Thank you again John, for arranging this, I am sure it will bring some peace to Margaret's soul," Sarah said.

"Thank you Sarah, for saying that. It brings me peace too. And how about you Sarah, how are you?" John asked in a friendly voice.

"I am good, and at a bit of a transition, where I am looking at how to move forward with my life, after all this disruption," Sarah answered.

And before John could respond to her, she asked, "Would you like to go for a walk, John? I have something to tell you."

Alarm bells were going off in John's head, wondering what on earth she was going to tell him.

"Yes of course, I am all ears, if there is something you wish to inform me of," John said staying calm and professional. They got up, went and changed their shoes and met back at the veranda. Sarah had informed Anna that they were going for a walk on her way back to the veranda, and Anna had wished her good luck.

"After you," John said as they left the veranda, "As you know the way around here." They headed off across the fields until they hit the path along a small stream.

"There is something I haven't told you, that I think you deserve to know," Sarah started. John's heart was racing faster in anticipation of what might be coming.

"After we returned from your cabin, I had an unexpected visitor knocking on my door one evening. A young man called James Hillman. I had no idea why he had come, and was hesitant to let him in, but he pleaded with me. So I took him straight through to my client room, next to the kitchen. And there, he confessed to me that he was the one who had run Margaret over that fatal night, and had then driven her to my house, by request of Margaret herself.

"It had been his 21st birthday; he had been way too drunk to drive home, but had not wanted his parents to know how drunk he was. And had not wanted to leave his brand new car behind, which had been a birthday present from his parents. He had been worried that his parents would have been angry with, him both for being drunk, and leave the car behind.

"So he had decided to take the car, not realising how drunk he had been until he was on his way. He couldn't live with his guilt anymore and decided to confess to me, and take whatever punishment would come his way. Which he left for me to decide," Sarah finished.

John burst out laughing, bent over, hit one hand on his knee and kept laughing so hard he had to hold his stomach in pain in the end. Not quite the reaction Sarah had expected, as she looked on in relief and amusement.

John eventually stopped laughing, glanced over at Sarah and started laughing again. Sarah waited patiently until he had finished and John sat down on a large stone. Sarah was relieved that John hadn't been mad at her for not telling him sooner, or that might be yet to come. She was just extremely surprised by his reaction.

So once he had sat down, she plucked up the courage to ask him, "What's so funny about this, John?"

"I'll tell you what is so funny, Sarah. For weeks, the mob and the police has been trying to work out who bumped Margaret off, worrying about who knew what. And all this time she got run over by a snotty, rich, twenty-one year old boy. I would not have believed it, if it had not come from you. So what have you decided, regarding this young man? And why didn't you tell me before?" John asked.

"To answer you last question first. I wanted you to sweat and worry, to punish you and the rest of the mob. One, because I thought you had something to do with it, from something Margaret told me that night. Secondly, to create suspicion amongst you all, because I thought you all deserved it. And I didn't know what to do with James Hillman, I needed time to think. That evening, when he told me the truth, I was so angry with him, I couldn't even look at him. And for a while I even thought that you had sent him to lie for you," Sarah explained.

"I see, thank you for explaining that to me. And out of curiosity, what did Margaret say to you that night, that made you think that I had tried to kill her?" John asked.

"Something about you had promised her, and she thought you must have changed your mind" Sarah replied.

"I see," John said slipping into his own thoughts.

"Did you plan to bump her off, John?" Sarah asked nervous about how he might react, but she had to know.

John could see that Sarah was nervous about asking him, and admired her for having the courage to do so anyway. He immediately wanted to put her at ease, as he didn't want her to be afraid of him; it was the last thing he wanted.

"No Sarah, the exact opposite. I had encouraged Margaret for a long time, to let me help her get away from the city and the life she was leading. I had offered to set her up somewhere new, far away from New York City. As a matter of fact, it was all set to go ahead that fatal night.

"I thought someone else got to her first, had tried to take her out, and had failed miserably in doing it with immediate effect. What Margaret had failed to tell me, was that she had two young sons, so that would have been a huge surprise, but still manageable.

"Knowing her, I cannot imagine her plan was to leave them behind. How she managed to keep them a secret from us all, I do not know. And my biggest regret right now, is that I didn't manage to persuade her sooner, in which case, she would still be alive, and those two beautiful boys would still have their mother.

"Towards the end, it was getting too dangerous what she was doing, trying to please everyone with more and more chance of someone finding out what she was doing."

Sarah had sat down too, while John had been talking, trying to take it all in and working it all out.

"So that's why, Margaret had seemed to hold John in high esteem, he had been helping her, offering her a way out."

"She was saying good bye," Sarah whispered.

"What was that?" John asked, as he hadn't quite heard what she had said.

"It makes sense now. Margaret was taking me out for dinner to say good bye to me," Sarah said, finally solving that part of the puzzle for herself.

"Since this might be the last time I get to see you, will you please allow me to explain my life to you?" John asked, feeling that this time Sarah would let him tell his life story.

"Okay," Sarah said calmly, ready to listen.

"I grew up in the house I live in now. My father was a very successful business man, mainly importing of goods. I was an only child and had a very happy childhood and loved my parents very much. They were my world. The mob had started putting pressure on my father to pay them protection money, but he refused every time the demands came.

"So eventually, they killed my parents and made their bodies disappear. I had been away at the time with Oscar and Rose, who worked for my parents back then. We didn't know what had happened; only that my parents had disappeared and all their assets ceased. We were given some story that my father had gone bankrupt and had disappeared along with my mother.

145

"Luckily, my father had feared that something like that could happen and had instructed Oscar and Rose in what to do. Oscar and Rose took me in, and my father had set up a trust fund for me, that Oscar was the trustee of. And we moved across town.

"I became an angry young man, after overhearing Oscar and Rose one day talking about what had probably happened to my parents. I got out of control, and started hanging out on the street in the mob neighbourhood, trying to be noticed by the mob, as someone who would do anything to become part of their organisation.

"The things I had to do to get to where I am now, I couldn't even begin to tell you. You would hate me for it. All I wanted to do was to find out what had happened to my parents and who had done it, and punish them. I was filled with hatred and anger, completely consumed by it.

"To begin with, it was an act, pretending not to care about the things I had to do, but eventually it became second nature. No one lived in my parent's house but the mob used it for meetings from time to time. And when eventually, I had earned enough money and status, I asked the mob if I could purchase the house. I told them I really liked it, and would take the previous owner's name as a joke as we were both Irish.

"The mob agreed and gave it to me for an anomaly fee, and they found it amusing, that one of them had bought the O'Connor house. Once I had established myself with the mob, which took a few years, I approached the police very carefully. I knew exactly which of the police was on the mob's payroll and who were not, telling them I wanted to work with them to take down the mob and brining my parent's killers to justice.

"It was risky, but I didn't care. And that's why I wanted to get Margaret away from it all, as I knew how dangerous it was. I am assuming that you know what Margaret did?" He asked.

"I only found out that night she died, before that, I had no idea," Sarah answered.

"So now you have the big picture, am I sure you might have many questions. But for now, let me say just this. I have told myself over and over again, that it has been worth it and justifiable. But I don't want it anymore; I don't think I ever really wanted any of it. It was the decision of a very angry young man, who was riddled with grief.

"What I would like is a normal happy life with the woman I love. So the only good thing that has come out of all of this is that I met you. I love you, Sarah."

It was more a statement than a declaration, and John was relieved to finally get it off his chest. Sarah was very quiet, taking it all in. Not so much John declaring his love for her, but his life story. She was so confused. Part of him was the man she had fallen for at the cabin, but he was also a mob member. Someone that had been involved in and done unspeakable things, in the name of avenging his parents. Could he ever leave that behind?

"Sarah, say something please," John pleaded.

"I don't know who you are, I don't even think you know who you are," Sarah said very quietly, still deep in her own thoughts.

"Well, I was hoping that I could figure that out together with you. If you will have me?" John replied to her statement.

"I can't deal with this right now, John. When I travelled up here, I had my whole future figured out, and it was good and peaceful. And then you show up again with your charm, your good looks and your kindness."

Sarah paused for a moment before she carried on.

"But however much you try to justify it, you did all those horrible things. I do feel sorry for what happened to your parents, and how devastating that must have been for you. But I don't think I can get past the way you chose to live your life for all those years." Sarah paused again.

"This has been a rollercoaster ride for me for so many reasons, but most of all, because you are the first man I have been remotely interested in since my husband died. And now I don't know what to do." Sarah was crying now.

"Even if I agreed, how could you ever leave the mob without them coming after you? How could you possibly keep us both safe, huh? Because I would really like to know." Sarah was pacing up and down now, really angry with herself, John, the world, with EVERYTHING!

"Sarah please calm down, I hate to see you in such distress," John said trying to calm her down by putting his hands on her shoulders.

"Get off me, you monster," Sarah shouted and wriggled herself free.

"My life was fine until you showed up, and I wish I had never clapped eyes on Margaret either," and with that she stormed off. John was beside himself, not for himself but for Sarah. He couldn't bear to see the pain she was in knowing it was nothing he could do about. In fact, knowing that he was the cause of it, made it even worse.

For a moment, he also wished they had never met, because then, Sarah would still be living her happy peaceful life. And he would not be feeling the way he was feeling right now. He thought it best to leave her alone for a while, and gave her a head start, and then walked slowly back to the farm.

Chapter Sixteen

When John arrived back on the farm, Anna, Ray, Henry and Thomas were sitting on the veranda, enjoying the warm evening.

"Evening all, Sarah not with you?" John asked.

"Sarah? I thought she was with you?" Anna said, looking worried. John didn't know what to say, and felt sick with worry.

"Where could she be? How could he explain?"

"I am afraid we had a disagreement and she went ahead of me," John said trying to sound calm.

"Don't worry, we will find her," Ray said cheerfully.

John could tell by Anna's look that she didn't trust him and was worried he had done something to Sarah.

"Jesus Christ, not Anna too!" He thought. It really began to dawn on him, how his lifestyle, effected normal decent folk. They were terrified of people like him.

Anna's thoughts were racing, "Oh my god, please let her be unharmed"

"We will help you look," Thomas said, and got up at the same time as Ray, and Henry followed. Henry had seen the look on Anna's face, and was now worried too. He had seen on the streets of New York, what people like John could do to people. And he didn't like seeing Anna upset, she was the best thing in his life now.

"I know where she will be," Ray said and walked off, closely followed by the two young brothers. This left Anna alone, with John.

"I would never harm her Anna, not in a million years. I love her," John said quietly and humbly. When Anna saw the look on John's face, she knew he was telling the truth and she relaxed.

"What did you say to her John that made her upset?" Anna asked.

"I told her my life story and that I love her and would like to share my life with her," John answered.

"No wonder she was upset, hearing about your line of business and trying to drag her into it," Anna said sarcastically.

"She didn't let me finish," was all John answered to that. But to himself he thought, "I, for sure, bring out the worst in these two gentle sisters, they don't need someone like me in their lives."

"What is taking them so long?" Anna asked herself.

"Could Sarah have harmed herself? How could she not have known how badly these events had affected Sarah; she should have known. And she should have supported her more. Sarah has always been the strong one, so I never worried about her. But this time I should have, I have really let her down."

"Do you want me to go have a look, as well," John asked Anna.

"No, I don't want you to get lost in the dark, thank you, there are no street lamps here you know!" Anna answered still being sarcastic and there was anger in there too. Ray and the boys had found Sarah down in the stables by her favourite horse, a large black stallion named Blacky.

Sarah loved him; he was so majestic with his shiny black coat, and his grounded calmness. And he was a good listener too.

"There you are," Ray said and smiled at her.

"Ray knew exactly where you would be!" Thomas said all excited.

Sarah had calmed down by now and said, "Yes, Ray knows where everything is on this farm," and smiled lovingly at her brother in law.

Both Henry and Thomas laughed at that, as they knew exactly what she meant. Ray knew something was up between Sarah and John, but considered it none of his business. Sarah seemed calm enough, but if John ever really upset his sister in law, there would be serious disagreement between them.

"Okay Sarah, let Blacky have some rest now, and you can have some nice herbal tea on the veranda," Ray said. Sarah smiled, because she knew what Ray was doing, and she loved him for it.

They all walked back to the veranda, happily chatting away, and Sarah avoided looking at John for the rest of the evening. And John left her alone; just glad she was back safe. And she seemed to have calmed down, which was a relief for him.

Ray and the boys went to bed fairly early, and Anna and Sarah cleared up and did the dishes, while John stayed on the veranda with a cigar. When Anna was ready for bed, she went out on to the veranda to get John and show him his room.

"Let me show you where you will be sleeping tonight, John," she said.

"Yes, thank you," he said and followed her.

As they said good night, Anna told him, "We are all up early, but don't worry, you can sleep as long as you wish. And if I am not around, you know where everything is in the kitchen," and with that she was gone.

She had been polite but guarded, and he couldn't blame her for that. It was a warm night and he felt restless, upset and worried about Sarah still, so he decided to go down to the kitchen and get himself a glass of water for the night stand.

As he filled his glass with water, he saw that Sarah was still on the veranda. He decided to go out and speak to her, hoping to make peace between them.

"Hi Sarah, may I sit down please?" He asked.

"Yes," she replied quietly, watching him sit down. "I do have a plan, a plan to leave my current life behind for good and never look back. It is safe and no one would ever find me. And I will do it with or without you, the choice is entirely yours," and with that he got up, said good night and went to bed.

Sarah enjoyed the slightly cool breeze on the veranda a little bit longer, then locked up and went to bed too. As she was lying in the dark trying to sleep, she remembered the knife jab she had felt in her heart when John had said, "I will do it with or without you."

She was tired of fighting her feelings for John and tired of judging him. If they could go somewhere new and start afresh, then she realised that that was what she wanted. She got up tip toed across the floor, opened her door quietly, tiptoed across the landing and opened John's bedroom door just as quietly.

She closed it quietly behind her, and stood still for a moment, not quite sure what she was doing. It had all been on impulse.

"Sarah?" She heard John say, and it was coming from the chair by the window. She had not noticed him there, as she thought he was in bed. Sarah froze.

"What are you doing here?" John asked very gently filled with excitement and worry.

"I don't know," Sarah replied whispering, suddenly feeling very nervous and stupid. She hadn't thought it through, before embarking on this little journey. John got up and walked slowly towards her and Sarah met him half way.

"Yes," was all she said.

"Yes what?" John asked as he took her in his arms and gently kissed her.

"Yes, I will share my life with you, but you will have to marry me," Sarah said in between kisses.

"Of course I am going to marry you," John replied.

"Did you really think I wasn't going to make an honest woman out of you?" He continued indignant.

"Just kiss me again, please John," Sarah said pleadingly.

"You have to go Sarah, I am not sure I can control myself," John pleaded.

"I don't want to, and you have already promised to make an honest woman out of me, the rest is just paper work," Sarah said teasingly, as she started to undress him and he helped her.

Then she pulled her night gown over her head and revealed her naked body. John gasped at the sight, lifted her up and put her on the bed. He kissed every part of her, from the top of her head to the bottom of her feet and ended up between her legs.

Sarah exploded and then let John in, and they were both lost in a passion unlike any other passion they had ever felt before. It was heightened by all the tension there had been between them and the control they had held on their feelings for so long. They felt that they finally were allowed to eat from the tree of the forbidden fruit. And that passion never left their relationship after that, for the rest of their lives they treasured what they had and how difficult it had been to get there.

Afterwards, Sarah fell asleep like a baby, wrapped in John's arms, the best sleep she had had in forever. John on the other hand, was so happy and excited he couldn't sleep. He just laid there with the woman he loved in his arms and a huge satisfied grin on his face. And eventually, he fell asleep too.

When Sarah woke up, she could feel John's manhood hard end erect up against her bum, and it immediately aroused her. She turned around and started to kiss a half asleep John, but it didn't take him long to be fully alert, rolled on top of her and entered her. Sarah was wet and ready for him and went into a heightened sense of consciousness and took John with her on the ride. It was quick, passionate and just as pleasurable as the night before, just different.

Afterwards John said, "I could get used to this," smiling from ear to ear.

"You better, because I will be demanding this daily," Sarah replied smiling too and cuddled up to him. If anyone had been standing outside looking in on them, they would say they both looked like the cat that got the cream.

"Mrs O'Connor, you are getting bossy already! I like it, you can boss me around anytime," John was teasing.

"You might regret those words Mr O'Connor!" Sarah teased back. Sarah then went back into her bedroom and had a quick wash and got dressed, while John was doing the same in his room.

Then they walked together down the stairs to have some breakfast. Anna was in the kitchen, already preparing lunch and knew full well that Sarah had stayed in John's room the night before, and didn't quite know where to look. Not because she was judging, Sarah was a grown woman, but because it was a bit awkward.

"Good morning to you both would you like breakfast or lunch?" she asked as naturally as she could.

"We might as well have lunch, as it is almost ready," Sarah answered, looking at John for approval.

"Fine with me," John said wanting to put his arms around Sarah again and never let her go. Now that they were out of his bed, he was frightened that Sarah might change her mind. And that last night and that morning, was a long moment of madness on her part. But he controlled himself out of respect for both women.

After lunch, Sarah asked John if they could go for a walk before he headed back to the city. John agreed, but again felt terrified that she was going to tell him she had changed her mind. As they walked across the fields for the second time, John took Sarah's hand and she willingly accepted.

"That's a good sign," he thought, and put his arm around her shoulder. And Sarah slipped her arm around his waist.

Sarah finally broke the silence, "How are you planning to break away John without causing suspicion, or put yourself in danger? And where are you planning to go? Is it somewhere you think I would like to live too?" John sighed a big sigh of relief.

"I will just slip away quietly, when no one is looking. And Oscar and Rose will raise the alarm when it is safe to do so. As in Margaret's case, the mob and the police will think I was bumped off. And my body will have been dumped where no one will find it.

"Oscar and Rose will stay for a while "mourning" me, and then decide to move on when it no longer looks suspicious for them to do so. My plan is to go to Dublin and to change my name too. Now, I know that is far away from your sister, but I feel that anywhere in America would not be safe. And in time, transatlantic flights will be common place and it wouldn't take you too long to go and visit your sister."

John went quiet, holding his breath, waiting for a response from Sarah.

"Dublin, Ireland," Sarah said tasting the words.

"It won't have the hot summers that we get here, but you won't get the cold snowy winters either. And if you really don't like it, we can move on," John added.

"Okay," Sarah had a million questions and wasn't sure where to start.

"So how will I slip away without looking suspicious?" She asked.

"You will sell your house and pack up, and the likelihood is that the police will not come and ask you why. If they do, you simply explain that after recent events you don't want to live in the city anymore. And if for any reason they should ask you where, just tell them you are going to stay with relatives for a while. They will buy it as you are a pure and innocent woman, who has been through a very hard time. But I very much doubt the police will have any interest in you from now on," John replied.

"In the meantime, I will get us new birth certificates and passports in our new names, and arrange for us to be married in the Old Dutch Church in Sleepy Hollow, so Anna and Ray can be there. Not the boys though, as it is better they don't know what we are up to. I will give you plenty of money, so you can buy yourself a dress with everything you need to go with it. And anything Anna and Ray might need, if they will accept any money from me."

Sarah started to look a bit worried, "Are you sure that nothing will go wrong John? I can't bear for anything to go wrong; after all we have been through."

John gave her a reassuring look, "I promise you, nothing will go wrong, and I know what I'm doing. I have been deceiving people for years and I am very good at it," John reassured her again.

"We will get married before you go back to the city, so that everything is ready to go, once you have organised the sale of your house. Unfortunately, I cannot help you with that, to be on the safe side. After our wedding, we should have no contact until we see each other again in Southampton, before heading for Dublin. I don't want anyone in Dublin to know that we came from America."

"Okay, it sounds as if you have it all worked out," Sarah said and felt a bit more relaxed, put her hands around John's neck and kissed him. When they got back to the farm, they told Anna that they needed to speak to her and Ray alone.

Anna fetched Ray and sent Henry and Thomas on an errand over to the neighbouring farm. Anna and Ray looked worried, as they thought something had gone wrong with the paper work regarding the boys.

It was silly of them to think that, as John hadn't even gone back to the city yet, but they couldn't think what else it could be. When they were all sat down comfortably on the veranda with a cold drink each, John started.

"Sarah and I are getting married and emigrating to Europe, as I don't wish to carry on with my current life. And need to go as far away as is safe for Sarah and me. And we would like for the two of you to be our witnesses," John finished.

Anna and Ray looked at Sarah and Anna asked, "Is this what you want, Sarah?"

"Yes, it is. I have been fighting my feelings for John for some time now, because I didn't think it was possible that we could be together. But now that I know that it is, there is nothing I want more," Sarah replied.

"Well, I haven't seen you smile like that in a very long time Sarah. You have my blessing," Ray said and turned to John and said, "If you ever upset her in any way again, I will row across the Atlantic and kick your arse."

John laughed, "I wouldn't expect anything less, and you have my word, I will make sure I never upset her ever again ever, so help me god!" Sarah looked at Anna, who hadn't spoken yet.

"I am happy for you; I can see that you really love each other. But will I ever see you again Sarah, once you leave?" Anna asked looking a bit concerned.

"Yes you will, I promise you. And we will speak on the telephone regularly," Sarah replied reassuring her sister.

"This calls for a celebration, come Sarah let's get some glasses," Anna said.

When the two sisters had gone Ray asked John, "What brought this on John?"

"The very first time I laid eyes on Sarah; I knew she was the woman for me. And ever since I have wanted out of my current life and building a new one with her. Even before I met Sarah, I had planned to leave my current life behind, she just gave me more of an incentive to do it sooner rather than later. I cannot imagine my life without her, and until last night I thought I would have to," John told Ray.

Ray looked at John and grinned, "I know exactly what you mean, when you see the woman for you, you know straight away. I felt exactly the same the first time I saw Anna.

"It wasn't easy as she was only sixteen and I was twenty one, and I didn't want anyone to think I was an old pervert. But I got her in the end and she makes me happy every minute of every day. And now thanks to you and Sarah, we have two lovely boys to call our own to complete our family, since we were never able to conceive our own children."

John smiled, "I am glad, and I hope that Sarah and I can make each other as happy as you and Anna make each other." John left for the city later that afternoon and his departure was as painful for him as it was for Sarah, maybe even more as she had her family around her. But he consoled himself with the fact that the next time he would see her would be at their wedding, the thought filled him with a happiness he had never felt before.

Within two weeks John and Sarah were married in the Old Dutch Church in Sleepy Hollow, a much happier occasion than the last time they were there. Sarah was wearing a full length slim fitted silk dress with a princess neckline covered in lace with all lace full length sleeves, and it had a small train at the back of the hem.

Her veil was beautiful lace, which was pulled tight over the middle of her head and tucked in behind her ears and reaching all the way to the floor and one yard behind her. Her blonde hair was beautifully finger waved at the front, and made into a sausage style bun at the back.

Her wedding bouquet was of medium size, with a flowing down effect with only lily of the valley in it, her favourite flower. John had opted for a very stylish day suit rather than the traditional morning coat, and the reason for that was that he didn't want to be discovered buying a wedding outfit as it could cause suspicion and he did not want to draw attention to himself at such a crucial time in his life.

He had to make sure that nothing went wrong, especially for Sarah's sake, but also for his own. No one would think anything of it, if he ordered himself a stylish new suit; it was something he did regularly. After all, they had both been through in their lives and the recent event around Margaret, they had been given a second chance, and he was going to make sure nothing would ruin that.

When John saw Sarah walking up the aisle on Ray's arm, he thanked god for giving him another shot at life, filled with love rather than anger. If he could help it he would make sure that this woman walking towards him would not have another day of misery for the rest of her life.

How they both felt that day, was an overwhelming sense of love and gratitude, which would stay with them for the rest of their lives together. Anna and Ray were absolutely thrilled too, seeing John and Sarah together that day, made them so very happy too.

They both realised that they had been secretly worrying about Sarah for years, living in New York on her own with no family around her, and no one to share her life with. After the love filled happy wedding ceremony, the four of them had a wedding meal in a quaint little restaurant nearby.

They were all happy and sad, as they knew that they wouldn't be able to get together again like that for a long time. After the meal they said their good byes, Anna and Sarah hugged and John and Ray shook hands both now considering the other a good friend.

John and Sarah spent their wedding night in pretty little guesthouse, signing in under their new names Karin and Karl Andersson.

"I wish I could have made this a much bigger and more extravagant occasion for you," John said to Sarah when they got to their room.

"Oh John, the whole day has been beautiful, I wouldn't have wanted it any other way," Sarah replied looking happy and content.

"It has been perfect."

"You are perfect Mrs Andersson, and I love you so much it hurts," John said and started undressing his bride. His longing for her the last couple of weeks had been unbearable, and he now just wanted to make love to her all night. They didn't get much sleep that night, they were too busy exploring each other's bodies, and finding out what gave the other, the most pleasure.

Having to part the next day not knowing exactly when they would see each other again, was terrifying for both of them. They were both acutely aware, that so many things could potentially go wrong, but they were both trying to hide their worry from the other.

John looked Sarah in the eyes and said, "Everything will go smoothly. I will make sure of it, and I will see you in Southampton very soon my darling Sarah. Just follow all the instructions I have given you, and remember if you are unsure about anything, make contact with Oscar and he will help you. I have explained to you how you can get to my house without being seen, and Oscar and Rose will not be alarmed if you should turn up unannounced. See you soon my love," was the last thing John said to Sarah before kissing his new bride.

Sarah waved him off and John could see her in his rear view mirror, and held that image in his mind for the next few weeks.

Chapter Seventeen

Sarah travelled back to Anna and Ray and stayed for a couple of more nights, making the most of her time with them. Especially her sister, as they had no idea when they would see each other again. She then returned to the city and started making arrangements for the sale of her house.

She knew she wouldn't get what the house had originally been worth, but it didn't matter as she didn't desperately need the money and wanted a quick sale. No one questioned her regarding selling up and moving away, which was a huge relief for her, and made it easier to pack up and leave.

She had arranged to ship some of her furniture and belongings, and had done it via Anna's and Ray's farm not to cause any suspicion. And after what had seemed like an eternity, she was on a ship heading for Southampton. John had got her a first class ticket, so she was very comfortable but had quite a bit of sea sickness for a couple of days.

Her cabin was lovely and her bed was very comfortable, but she missed John terribly, especially at night. In the dining room she was put on a table with some wealthy English people, and one particular lady had been very chatty, but also a bit too nosy for Sarah's liking.

She didn't want anyone to know anything about her, and to forget her as soon as she was off the ship. At one point the English lady, and she actually was a real lady, Lady Hampton had said she was sure she recognised Sarah from New York and had asked her which part of New York she was from.

Sarah had given Lady Hampton just enough information to quell her curiosity, by saying she was originally from Sweden, but now lived in Dublin and had just been visiting relatives in America.

Thankfully, Lady Hampton seemed satisfied with her answer, and had left Sarah alone after that, as she had realised that Sarah didn't have any status, just money. So Sarah became someone of no significance to Lady Hampton.

"Thank god for English aristocracy snobbery," Sarah thought, "Because that has just saved me from further investigation." She laughed inside and thought, "John will be proud of me the way I handled that, I am becoming as good at deceiving others as he is. Or maybe not as professional as him at it, but give me time," she said to herself and laughed inside again.

They had a couple of days of strong winds with medium size waves, and the slow rolling up and down, made Sarah sea sick. She felt dizzy and as if she wanted to throw up but couldn't, all she could do was lie on her bed, and praying it would end soon.

And so, desperately wishing John was there with her, she felt she could cope with anything when he was by her side. Her strong, handsome considerate husband, which she loved so much.

After a couple of days, the wind died down and Sarah was able to get up and join the others for some food in the dining room. She was starving after not having eaten for two days. She had scrambled eggs, beans and toast, with a delicious cup of tea.

Food had never tasted so good, and the food had been of a very high standard throughout the whole journey.

"Glad to see you up and about again Mrs Andersson," Lady Hampton said in a slightly more frosty tone than before, as she now considered herself way above Sarah in society. This suited Sarah fine, as there would be no more interrogation from Lady Hampton.

The last couple of days before they reached Southampton, the weather was lovely and Sarah very much enjoyed standing or sitting on deck all day, just watching the sea. As they docked in Southampton, she was ready packed and standing on the deck where she could see the crowd on the dock, waiting for their friends, family and loved ones.

She spotted John almost straight away amongst the crowd, and her heart skipped a beat. She was so happy to see him; she couldn't wait to get off the ship. John saw Sarah and waved, looking at her with that big beautiful smile of his.

She had been so worried that something would happen to him before she got there, and he would not be able to meet her. When she came off the plank John ran towards her, lifting her up swinging her around and holding her so tight she could hardly breathe.

"Am I happy to see you Mrs Andersson. It feels like a lifetime since I saw you last. Let's go and find your luggage and get on the next train to London," he

said and grabbed her hand heading for the arrivals terminal. She got through pass
port control okay with her Swedish passport, they only asked her one question
and that was how long she would be in the UK.

She answered a couple of weeks maximum, and the immigration official
seemed happy with her answer. They managed to get on the next train heading
for London, and John had got them tickets in first class. There weren't that many
people in first class, so they managed to find themselves two seats away from
the other passengers, which gave them the privacy they wanted.

After their initial embrace and the hustle and bustle of the arrivals terminal,
they both suddenly felt a little bit shy in each other's company. They had been
separated for quite a few weeks and they hadn't yet established their new
intimate relationship.

So, for most of the journey, they sat quietly next to each other, John with his
arm around Sarah, and Sarah leaning her head on his shoulder. When they arrived
at Victoria station in London, John got a porter to deal with Sarah's luggage and
lead them to the black cab stand in front of the station.

John told the driver they were going to The Savoy, and off they went. The
journey took them past Buckingham Palace, through The Mall and Trafalger
Square and down The Strand to the Savoy Hotel, which was the only place in
London where they drove on the right hand side entering the hotel area.

Sarah really enjoyed the views, she had seen pictures of London, but it was
way more exciting to be there. John was watching her and smiled at her familiar
childlike wonder when she enjoyed something. They were almost home and dry
now, just a few things for him to sort out here in London. And he wanted to show
Sarah a good time while they were there, to make up for the courtship they had
never really had.

Since he had already checked in days ago, all Sarah had to do was sign the
register and show her passport, and then they could finally be alone. Once they
were in the room and John had paid the bell boy a tip, they just looked at each
other smiled and started kissing. They ripped each other's clothes off and fell on
the bed, where John entered Sarah straight away.

She didn't mind, as she wanted it just as much as him. Once round one was
over, and they had satisfied that desperate first need for each other, they slowed
down and explored each other's bodies again, as they had done before. Now that
the initial awkwardness had gone, they could fully appreciate each other in every
way.

And that first evening they didn't want to leave the room, and eventually ordered room service for their dinner. Sarah loved the room which had a view of the river Thames, the whole hotel was so beautiful and luxurious, and she was completely blown away.

John was really spoiling her, and when she told him so, he smiled and said, "Only the very best for my beautiful darling lady wife," and he really meant it. And from that day onward he always called her my darling, which was also easier than remembering to call her Karin.

Sarah was everything to him and if he could give her the moon and the stars, he would. There were a few things that Sarah wished to do while in London, top of her list was Kew Gardens. And they spent a lovely afternoon there, enjoying all the exotic plants and the Chinese Pagoda and the quaint little palace which among other British monarchs had been home to George III after he became mentally ill.

And they had enjoyed the traditional afternoon tea in a pretty little café in the nearby small town of Richmond. The tiny white sandwiches with the crust cut off, and the tiny little cakes was a very different experience from the delis in New York that they were used to. Sarah loved it all.

Every new experience made her forget about what they had been through in the last few months, since Margaret's death. They repeated the experience of afternoon tea at the Fortnum & Mason, one of the oldest department stores in London, situated on the street Piccadilly.

Sarah enjoyed it just as much the second time as she had done the first time, and liked the fact that the cakes were slightly different as well. The scones she wasn't that keen on and left them for John to eat.

She knew he didn't enjoy it as much as her and that it probably wasn't enough food for him. But John enjoyed anything that Sarah enjoyed, as it made him happy to see her happy. She had given up a lot for him and she was a long way from home.

So he wanted her to enjoy every little bit that she could, until they hopefully would settle in Dublin. John had some paper work that had to be dealt with before they could depart for Ireland, and he didn't want to bore Sarah with public office visits, and told her to go explore on her own.

Sarah had heard of Madame Tussauds when she was a young girl, and was curious to go and see what all the fuss was about. She didn't like it at all; she found the wax sculptures a bit creepy. So she walked through as quickly as she could.

It was the only disappointment she had had in London so far, so she didn't mind so much. The question was, what she would do with herself until she was going to meet up with John again back at the hotel. She could see from the map she had with her that Regents Park was literally just behind the museum, and decided to go for a walk there.

She was surprised how beautiful it was, a pearl, literally in the centre of London. She walked around the lake, and then headed back to Baker Street station, where she got on a bus which would take her to Knightsbridge and the famous department store, Harrods.

She went to the upstairs deck of the bus where she could see the views much better. They went down Baker Street and passed Selfridges as they turned right on to Oxford Street, and she made a mental note that she would like to visit Selfridges as well before they left, another Famous department store.

She had never been much of a shopper, but she found these English department stores fun to visit. They had so much history, and the staff was incredibly polite and helpful, and she absolutely loved their English accent.

They turned left off Oxford Street at Marble Arch and on to Park Lane, where she passed two very new hotels, the Dorchester and the Grosvenor House.

And on her right hand side was Hyde Park, "What a treat," she thought, "For the price of a bus ticket I get to see all this." She was very happy with herself; the day had turned out very well after all. Harrods was a great experience too, with its amazing food halls and china and glass department.

After Harrods, she jumped on a bus back to the hotel, which took her down Piccadilly past The Ritz, another grand hotel in London, and she got to see Fortnum & Mason again too.

She passed the Royal Academy of Arts and the famous Piccadilly Circus, after that the bus then went down Haymarket, through Trafalger Square where the National Gallery was situated, passed Charing Cross station and the bus pretty much stopped outside the hotel.

She rushed into the lobby heading for the lifts as she was late back to meet up with John. John had been worried when Sarah was not back at their agreed time, and was pacing up and down in the hotel lobby by the time Sarah got there. She was surprised to see him in the lobby and not in the room.

When he saw her, his face changed from worry to relief, but he wanted to reprimand her for being late and making him so worried. But when he saw how happy she was he just couldn't do it.

She was so excited about the fact that she had passed so many famous landmarks on her journey around London that day, and was telling him as they walked to the lifts.

John's heart completely melted from her excitement, so when Sarah finally apologised for being late he just said, "Don't worry my darling; I am just so glad you had a good time."

John had completed all the business he needed to get done in London, and asked Sarah if there was anything else she wanted to do or see in London before they headed for Ireland.

She looked a bit embarrassed as he had already spoiled her so much, but did say she would like to visit Selfridges. If my darling wife wants to see Selfridges she shall, I will take you there tomorrow and we can have afternoon tea again.

"Oh how exciting," Sarah said and clapped her hands. John smiled and gave her a hug and they ended up making love again for the third time that day. So on their last day in London they headed for Selfridges, after a lazy morning in bed followed by breakfast in the room.

They had meant to go to the theatre a couple of times, but had always ended up in the hotel restaurant where the food was so excellent they couldn't resist it, so they had not bothered to go looking for other restaurants or entertainment, they were more interested in entertaining each other in bed.

And each evening after dinner they had headed straight back to the room for more intense devouring love making.

At Selfridges they had had their final afternoon tea in London and John had treated Sarah to several new outfits. And before dinner they had packed everything ready for the journey to Liverpool the next day. They had quite a bit extra to pack, as they had done some food shopping in Fortnum & Mason. Mainly tea of all different kinds, as that was Sarah's favourite drink.

The next morning, they got a black cab to Liverpool Street Station and got on the train to Liverpool where they would catch the steamship to Dublin. It was a long train journey, so John had booked them into a hotel in Liverpool for one night before heading to sea and Dublin.

They had both fallen in love with Dublin from day one, and they found a house they both liked on the outskirts of the city on a quiet street. John took his time setting up his business, which was mainly import of household goods, as he didn't want anyone to think he had a lot of money and wondering how he had obtained that kind of cash.

The first letter Sarah received from Anna had an absolutely beautiful and very much unexpected surprise in it. Anna was pregnant! After all these years of hoping for a baby, the doctor had said that now that she had finally given up, she had relaxed and her body had cooperated. And she had three men fussing over her the entire pregnancy.

Of course, Anna and Ray were over the moon and surprisingly enough Henry and Thomas were really excited too. The following August, Anna gave birth to a beautiful baby girl and they named her Elizabeth after Anna and Sarah's mother with Margaret as her middle name, honouring Henry and Thomas's birth mother.

Sarah was so very happy for her sister and wanted to go and see her, but then discovered that she was pregnant herself. John had thought that he couldn't be happier than he already was, but when Sarah told him she was pregnant, he was ecstatic.

It had never occurred to him that they might have children, but now they were going to, he felt his life was complete. Their first born was a boy and they named him William after John's father, and they were also blessed with a second child, a little girl who they named Alice.

They chose the name Alice because it was Swedish, and they were now "the Andersson's" and they both liked it. Anna and Sarah had been in constant contact, and when William and Alice were a little bit older, Sarah had been to visit Anna and her family on two occasions.

And Sarah was still so happy that Anna now had the family she deserved. It would have been very hard to leave the country and live so far away if Anna and Ray had still been on their own.

Henry and Thomas completely doted on their little sister Elizabeth, who was spoiled rotten by them all, but nobody minded. And Elizabeth was a kind and generous little girl, taking after her mother. And she didn't seem negatively affected by being so spoiled all the time.

Thomas was a natural farmer and really clear he wanted to take over the farm one day, and Ray was absolutely delighted by that. He would never have forced either of the boys to take over the farm if they had not wanted to.

Henry, on the other hand, the serious responsible one, wanted to be an attorney. And with Ray's savings and the trust fund from John, he could definitely fulfil his dream. He was a very clever and intelligent young man.

Chapter Eighteen

Twenty years later, on a warm summer's evening, John was sitting on his porch enjoying a cigar. Even at fifty six he was still a very handsome man. He was still slim and had not yet got much grey hair, not that it showed anyway as he had always been very blonde, so the grey blended in nicely.

He thought back on his life and what a lucky escape he had had. Back in 1932 when he had planned his escape from New York and the mob, one little mistake could have cost him his life, and put Sarah in danger. Because of Margaret's carelessness, he was at risk of being found out too.

That was one of the reasons he had wanted to get her away from New York, to protect himself. He had accomplished the promise he had made to himself when he was sixteen, and by the time he had met Sarah he had already been planning the escape for a while. And originally, Sarah had been another obstacle depending on how much she knew.

It had taken him years to find out who had "taken care" of his parents, and the ones responsible had been severely dealt with before being killed by him. He had never been proud of the fact that he had been capable of such an act, but at the time he had been able to justify it.

Unfortunately, it had not had the effect on him that he had wished for, quite the opposite. He had lowered himself to their standards, and instead of feeling that justice had been done, he felt disgust for himself. And had settled into that life even more, thinking there was no way out, after that.

And he had carried on fucking up the mob as much as he could at all times. And then he had met Sarah, who had brought out the best in him. She had been like a breath of fresh air, with her honesty and innocence. Not to mention her elegance and beauty, she had to him represented everything that was good in the world. And more than ever he had wanted to get away from his then life for good, and he wanted Sarah to come with him.

He had to laugh to himself, as that bit had not been easy. He remembered that gorgeous trip that they had taken up to his cabin by Lake Oscaleta, what a beautiful place that had been. If there was anything he missed from America it was that place, and his cabin.

They had, for the most part, had an amazing time, and Sarah had taught him about the spirit world and his parents had communicated with him. Or had they? He had never been entirely sure about that, it had probably only been his imagination that had run wild, that day.

At the time he had felt that Sarah had enjoyed his company and trusted him, but when they had got back to New York the shit had hit the fan. Sarah had had a complete break down for a couple of days, not surprisingly after what she went through with Margaret that fatal night.

And she completely turned on him, thinking he was the devil and he had got Margaret killed. Even thinking about it twenty years later was painful, and at the time he had almost admitted defeat. He had pretty much prepared himself for leaving America behind alone.

As even after Margaret's intimate funeral in Sleepy Hollow with her boys Henry and Thomas and their future adoptive parents, Anna and Ray, Sarah's sister and brother in law, had failed to win Sarah over.

At that point, he remembered that he had actually given up, and was planning his new life without her. But fate had brought them together one more time at Anna's and Ray's farm, when he had travelled up to the farm with some paper work regarding the boys, which had had to be signed.

And he had finally been able to tell Sarah his life story, to at least have her think a little bit better of him. He had made a life choice as a sixteen year old grieve stricken teen ager, and had to live with the consequences of that for the rest of his life.

He stilled looked over his shoulder from time to time, making sure he hadn't been found out, and they were coming for him. Would he ever be able to escape his past, he wondered? He had never shared with Sarah how worried he had been for their safety when they first settled in Dublin, or that he still worried from time to time.

He considered it his job to keep her safe and happy, something he had also promised Ray all those years ago. Sarah and their children were the absolute best things that had happened to him in his life, and he would not let any of them down.

Even if it would cost him his life to keep them safe, he would do so. He remembered the relief he had felt when Sarah had told him about James Hillman, the young man who had confessed to running Margaret over and consequently, killing her.

For him that had meant that none of the mob had been on to Margaret, which had kept him safe, long enough to get away. He had chosen Swedish names for them, because they could both easily have been Scandinavian by looks.

The best memory he had was of the night at Anna and Ray's farm after his and Sarah's long talk, Sarah's upset and they having finally made some peace, before they went to bed. He had been sitting by the window in the room he was to sleep in, at the farm, when Sarah had walked through the door.

She had finally given into her feelings for him and had decided not to deny herself a second chance at happiness, even if it was with a soon to be ex mob member. The passion and the love they had both felt that night had been out of this world, and had always stayed with them.

Even now, twenty years later, they made love pretty much every night, they simply could not keep their hands off each other. Which their children found a huge embarrassment, but secretly they also loved it that their parents had so much love for each other.

For obvious reasons, William and Alice did not know their parents originally came from New York, they had been told that they were from Sweden. And Sarah and himself had secretly learned enough Swedish to get away with that story, and luckily for them, like most children, they had not been interested in learning the parents mother tongue.

Unfortunately, he had not seen Oscar and Rose again once he had left New York which had saddened him often. Rose had had a terrible journey getting to America and would not brave the seas again. But John had been able to speak to them a few times over the years until they both had passed away.

As John was sitting there reminiscing, a very well dressed young man walked up his garden path, looking very serious. John got up to greet him, immediately on guard, wondering who he could be. They didn't receive many unexpected guests.

"Hello John, how are you?" The young man said.

"John?" Nobody had called him that in public for over twenty years. He began to feel very nervous. Had that moment he had feared, for twenty years, finally arrived? He was trying to suss out the young man, was he dressed like a mob member?

Not really, but that could be a disguise. Did he look like he was carrying a weapon? No.

John relaxed a little bit and said, "Can I help you? As there is no one by that name here."

"Don't you recognise me? I'm Henry, Anna and Ray's son," Henry replied.

"Henry, oh my god, what a pleasant surprise, come and sit down. But call me Karl, as that is the name I go by now. Karl Andersson," John said.

"Yes I eventually heard about yours and Sarah's great escape," Henry said grinning. Henry had grown very tall at least six foot two inches, with thick dark brown curly hair, and a very good physique. And there was something very solid and serious about him, but in a good way.

"I had planned to come and visit while I served in England towards the end of the war," Henry continued.

"But I didn't get much leave, and when I was released from service, I wanted to go straight home to see my family on the farm."

"Yes of course, I totally understand that, so what brings you here now Henry?" John asked.

"Well, over the years, I have overheard Anna and Ray talk about my mum Margaret from time to time, and eventually asked them to spill the beans. But they always claimed they didn't know much, apart from that there had been a terrible hit and run accident. And if I wanted to know more I would have to ask you and Sarah. So here I am and I have questions I would like answered," Henry looked John straight in the eyes, "And don't even think of lying to me or shelter me from the truth."

John smiled gently; he had, in fact, expected that this day would come. He also thought how much Henry looked like his birth mother Margaret, which was strangely comforting.

"What would you like to know Henry? I am happy to answer any questions you might have, and some of the answers, I will ask you to keep confidential."

"Yes that is not a problem, I just want to know the truth for myself and Thomas, if he is interested," Henry replied.

"Was my mother's death, an accident?" Henry asked.

"Yes it was, it was a hit-and-run by a young man at the time called James Hillman, who later confessed to Sarah," John answered.

170

"What did my mother do for a living?" Henry carried on.

"She was an informant for the mob, then later on she also became an informant for the police," as John finished that sentence, he could see the relief on Henry's face.

"What did you think she did?" John asked Henry.

"Well, some of the women who used to babysit us thought she was a prostitute, but I didn't know what that meant back then. I just overheard the women gossiping," Henry replied.

"She was gone all hours, and she obviously couldn't tell them what she really did, so I guess I can't blame them for thinking what they did," Henry added.

"Yes, she was playing a dangerous game, and did it to support herself, you and Thomas," John said.

"Yes, but the thing is John, why didn't you, who claimed to be her friend, help her escape that life? Why did you wait until she was dead, to just help Thomas and myself?" Henry looked angry now, wanting to blame John for losing his real mother.

"I tried to talk her into it many times, but she refused to accept my help for a long time. And I didn't know about you and Thomas, she had kept that from all of us, and came as a complete shock and surprise to me and Sarah at the time. How she managed to keep the two of you a secret from everyone, I don't know, but she did. And the night she got run over and died, was the night I had arranged her disappearance, and instead that tragic accident happened. I am truly sorry that I didn't manage to persuade her to leave sooner, I really am Henry," John said sincerely.

"She was a good woman, and a very loving caring mother, and I still miss her," Henry said.

"Yes I agree, and she was a very strong and resourceful woman. But unfortunately, she was also stubborn as a mule, which in the end, I believe was her downfall. Had she acted sooner, when she first had the chance, she would probably still be alive today," John wished he hadn't added that last bit, but it was too late to take it back.

Henry had calmed down and was deep in thought, and seemed to have had all his questions answered. But then he asked, "What happened to James Hillman?"

John, was startled by the question, but also understood why Henry asked.

"Nothing," John answered.

"Why?" Henry asked outraged.

"Because it would have drawn a lot of attention from the mob and the police, and it would have drawn attention to you and Thomas. So Sarah and I decided to leave it to keep you and Thomas safe, and also Anna and Ray," John said, and he was really clear that they had made the right decision back then.

Henry went silent for a long while and then said more to himself than to John "I could go looking for him; he probably wouldn't be hard to find. But I guess that could still put you and Sarah in danger, which I, of course, do not wish to do. Not just you and Sarah, but William and Alice too. Since no one of importance back then knew Thomas and I existed, it is pretty pointless. Apart from, I can't help but think that, that man never had to pay for what he did."

"Believe, you mean, and I speak from experience, he would live with the image of your mother's battered body every day of his life. He would never be able to escape his own thoughts and memories of what he caused," John said.

Henry's face was now twisted in pain and he asked, "Were they really bad, her injuries?"

John nodded, "I'm afraid so, Sarah still sometimes has nightmares about the state of Margaret that night. I am telling you this, not to upset you, but because I sense that you want the whole truth however ugly it might be. And you are a grown man who has been to war, and have probably seen a lot of gory things by now," John replied.

Henry looked very serious and said, "Thank you for being so honest with me, I respect that, it is not always easy to speak the truth. You are a good man John; I have always known that, how you ended up in the mob I do not know. And I guess I will never know, or will I?" He said looking at John inquisitively.

"Well, as we are being completely honest with each other, and this is a confidential conversation, I will tell you my story," John answered.

"I was sixteen and my parents disappeared without a trace, I was devastated. And through listening in on my two guardians whenever I could, I found out that the mob had got rid of them because my father would not pay protection money. I swore revenge from that moment on, and did everything to become part of the mob so that I could find my parents killers"

"Did you find them?" Henry asked.

"Yes I did," John replied.

"And what did you do with them?" Henry asked, now really intrigued by the whole story. John smiled at Henry's eagerness to find out the details, and recognised the need in Henry for revenge for his mother.

"Very bad things, which I have had to live with for more than thirty years, and I don't recommend it. You think you are going to feel better, but I promise you Henry, you won't."

"I think I already know that," Henry said. John smiled,

"What a fine young man Henry was and so wise, Margaret would have been so proud."

"Why are you smiling, John?" Henry asked.

"I was thinking what a fine, wise young man you have turned out to be, your mother would have been so proud."

"Thank you for saying that John, it really means a lot," Henry said and started to sob quietly.

"You let it out boy, I know exactly how you feel," he thought, and it brought him back to that night on the jetty by his cabin when he had finally released his pain of losing his parents, greatly thanks to Sarah's presence at the time.

When Henry stopped sobbing, John said, "There are lots of ways you can honour your mother without seeking revenge. You could set up a charity to raise money for struggling single mothers, or being an attorney you can make it your life's works that there is justice for everyone. That no one get away with murder, literally."

Henry was smiling now, "Yes, you are right; my mother would have much preferred one of those options. I think I will take on both, as one does not exclude the other."

John felt so happy that Henry had come to see him, and that he had managed to give this young man some closure on the past, and a fulfilling future to live into.

"How is Thomas?" John asked. The mention of his brother's name put a big smile on Henry's face.

"Oh you know Thomas; he is so wonderfully uncomplicated. He loves being a farmer, he loves life and he has always brought so much joy to Anna and Ray. He married one of the local farm girls, and couldn't be happier.

"And they have three children already, but you probably knew that?" Henry answered.

"And what about you Henry, are you happy, and is there a special woman in your life?" Henry smiled a big smile now.

"As it happens there is, she is English and that is why, I am over here. I am getting married in London next week and I was hoping you would be my best man," Henry said.

John was completely taken by surprise. Not by the fact that Henry was getting married, but by his request for him to be the best man.

"You want me to be your best man? I feel deeply honoured. But what about Thomas or Ray, surely one of them should be your first choice?"

"I must admit they both were, but neither of them is willing to cross the Atlantic, and I cannot think of a better third choice than you," Henry said with a sheepish look on his face.

"Don't feel bad," John said after noticing the sheepish look on Henry's face.

"I am more than happy to be third choice, and I know Sarah will be made up too. Both that you are getting married and that you have chosen me to be the best man," John said.

"Oh good, that's settled then," Henry said with a huge smile on his face.

"Where is Sarah by the way?" Henry asked.

"Oh, she went into town with William and Alice to get them some new clothes, before they start there autumn term. And by the way, please make sure you call me Karl, and Sarah Karin in front of William and Alice, as they have no idea about our real past, and I would like to keep it that way."

"Yes of course, your secrets are safe with me I guarantee you that," Henry reassured John.

"Thank you, I very much appreciate that," John replied. He had no more said those words when Karin, Alice and William came walking up the garden path. All three were very curious who this handsome young man was, sitting on the porch talking with Karl.

"Can you guess who this is Karin?" Karl asked Karin.

"Of course I can. Hi Henry, how wonderful it is to see you again," she said walking over to Henry giving him a big hug.

"You can't fool this woman," Karl said with a big smile on his face, giving Karin a hug and a passionate kiss.

"Dad, do you have to be so embarrassing, when we have got company," William said, and turned to Henry and shook his hand and said, "So nice to see you again Henry, it has been years."

Henry shook William's hand, smiled and said, "Likewise, really good to see you too William."

Alice felt a bit shy in front of this handsome grown man, and said, "Hi Henry, nice to see you, how is Elizabeth?"

"Really well thank you, she sends her love, they all send their love," Henry replied.

"Have you offered Henry a drink Karl?" Karin asked.

Karl gave her a guilty look, and turned to Henry and said, "I am so sorry Henry, what kind of host and best man, am I," he said and winked at Henry.

"Best man? Are you getting married? Who is she, and where and when is this taking place?" Karin was all excited.

"In London next week, Ray and Thomas didn't fancy the journey, and I have to have some family there. So I hope you are all coming," Henry said.

"Mum, can we?" Alice pleaded.

"Of course we are all coming, aren't we, Karl?" she still managed to say that name with a bit of a Swedish accent which really amused John. Sarah had turned out to be a great actress, who could lie with great conviction, John had found out over the years. He still got the same butterflies in his stomach every time he looked at her, Sarah had kept on surprising him over the years, with how strong, and quick thinking and smart she was.

"But tell me Henry, who is this lucky woman who gets to spend her life with you?" Karin asked.

"A beautiful and smart English rose called Louise; we met while we both were working for the foreign office in London. She is an attorney, just like me, and she has finally agreed to marry me and move to New York," he pulled out a picture from his pocket and it was passed around.

"What a beauty," William said and whistled.

"William," Karin was shocked, "Behave yourself, that is your cousin's future wife you are referring too," she said looking really crossed.

"Don't worry, I take it as a compliment," Henry said, and added with a smile, "She wouldn't look twice at you, anyway." And William just laughed back at him.

"This is really cause for a celebration, let me get some champagne and some glasses. Will you help me Karl?" Karin said.

"Yes of course, my darling," Karl replied and got up and they both disappeared into the house. Later on, when they were all having supper together,

Sarah was looking around the table thinking how lucky she was. And remembering what it had taken to get to where they were now.

Thinking about all the twists and turns she and John had been through, before she had finally admitted to herself that she really loved him and didn't want to live without him. It had not been without risk, and there were a couple of times it could have gone really badly.

One thing that had worried her back in New York, before she had left for England, had been James Hillman. At the time she had thought what if he had gone to the police himself and confessed?

They would then have questioned her, why she had not told the investigation what she knew. It could have gotten really ugly, so thank god James Hillman had kept his mouth shut, and saved his own skin, because he had also saved hers.

And of course she had let it slip that Margaret had children in her rage towards James Hillman, which he could also have revealed. This would have put Henry and Thomas in danger too.

She had occasionally wondered how no one had seen the accident or what happened after, and had thought that maybe the police and James's father had known. And the father had paid off the police to keep it quiet, as they didn't want anything to be known about Margaret either.

Mr Hillman had protected his son, and the corrupt police Margaret had been working for, had protected themselves. But these were just speculations and she would never know if she was right. And luckily no one had questioned why she had wanted to leave the city, so the sale of the house had gone smoothly.

There had been that one incident on the ship on her crossing over the Atlantic, where the English Lady had thought she recognised her, but Sarah had managed to convince her otherwise.

She had never regretted making the decision to be with John and settling in Dublin, they had been so very happy from the start, and they still were extremely happy. Not that many people were blessed with a long and happy marriage, but John made her feel loved and happy every day.

The only regret in all of it had been that she had had to leave her sister and family behind. But she had been busy with her two lovely children that she had been blessed with, and she did the occasional reading and had carried on with her meditation and communicating with spirit when she had some spare time.

William, who now was at university studying English literature and history, was the spitting image of his father, tall blonde blue eyed, with the same cheeky

176

in. He had a very outgoing personality, who liked to have fun and hanging out with his friends. But John and Sarah made sure he took his studies seriously.

Alice, who was still in High school, was a mix of John and Sarah, and more of an introvert. She, wanted to be a lawyer like her cousin Henry and work on women's rights, which was much needed in catholic Ireland, she believed.

Her eyes were not blue nor green they were somewhere in between, very unusual and striking, and she too had inherited the blonde hair. Both Alice and her brother were tall, taking after their parents. When you saw the four of them together, there was no doubt that they were a family.

Sarah, while sitting at the table watching them all, thought of Margaret, and was really sad that she had had to "sacrifice" her life, to bring so much happiness o herself and her sister Anna. And from what John had told her, Margaret's eath was still haunting Henry after all these years.